THE
RABBI
WHO KNEW
TOO MUCH

David Y Kopstein

The Rabbi Who Knew Too Much
Copyright © 2015 David Y Kopstein

This is a work of fiction. The people, corporations, organizations, institutions, circumstances, and events depicted are fictitious and a product of the author's imagination. Any resemblance of any character to any actual person, either living or dead, is purely coincidental.

ISBN 13: 978-1-59298-840-2

Library of Congress Catalog Number: 2015914296

Printed in the United States of America

First Printing: 2015

19 18 17 16 15   5 4 3 2 1

Cover and interior design by Laura Drew.

Beaver's Pond Press
7108 Ohms Lane
Edina, MN 55439–2129
952-829-8818
www.beaverspondpress.com

To my grandchildren—Aviva, Benjamin Zev, Elimeleḥ, Ḥannah,
Isaac, Judah, Leeba, Naḥman, Rivka, Ruben, the one on the way—
and the generations to come.

INTRODUCTION

W e're all connected to the past in some way. No one has
come into this world entirely by accident. We've all arrived
because of our ancestors' critical decisions—and a greater or lesser
degree of their good fortune.

The Jewish tie to the past is somewhat more noted than usual.
Although scattered to "the four corners of the earth," Jews have always formed a cohesive and fairly literate group. As a result, much
of their backstory has been chronicled for them.

From the Five Books of Moses, it is an easy step to the succes-
sion of priests and Levites of the Temple of Jerusalem, and from
there, to the Jews of Babylonia and Rome. Jews prayed in the synagogues of Rome well before Christianity came on the scene; Ju-
lius Caesar was their neighbor. From there, it is a short journey to
southern France and northeast Spain, thence to central and eastern Europe, and ultimately to modern Israel and America.

What unfolds on these pages is an attempt to transmit a portion of that history in the form of a fictional memoir. Although
most of what you are about to read actually happened in one way
or another, some of the names and dates have been changed "to
protect the innocent."

My inspiration comes from the words of poet Joan Walsh An-
glund, which I have modified to apply to this composition: "A bird

doesn't sing because it has great wisdom to impart; it sings because it has a song."

We might say that what follows are the words of my song.

Rabbi David Kopstein
Kailua-Kona, Hawaii

PART I

IN AND OUT OF A DREAM

CHAPTER I.

 SINGAPORE. NOVEMBER 2007.

Time moves in one direction, memory in another.
WILLIAM GIBSON

"Riverside Hotel, please."

"Riverside. Yes, yes, yes," the Singaporean cabdriver shot back in rapid-fire jabber.

I could tell I was in for a wild ride. Standing on the curb just outside the baggage claim area, I leaned into the open passenger window and made my usual precautionary request. "I need to sit up here next to you," I told the driver, rubbing my stomach to feign illness. "I get carsick."

It was true. On long road trips back in the late '50s, before the interstate highway system was completed, the entire Kadison family quickly learned we were best off with me in the front seat, near the passenger window. As she moved over to the middle of that long front seat to make room for me, my mother would always whisper to me, "You'll never make it as an astronaut, son." The new seating arrangement solved the problem, and more than that. Having found the remedy for car sickness, I began to develop an incurable travel bug.

My mother was right, of course. I never did become an astronaut. But I was often accused of having my head in the clouds. And I managed to fly around the world more than once. And over the next half century, I accumulated enough air miles to make it to the moon and back, twice.

Now look at me, I told myself as I opened the taxi door. *A neighborhood runt from the old North Side, now world citizen Rabbi Jonathan Jacob Kadison—spiritual leader of the Progressive Hebrew Congregation of Auckland, New Zealand—overnighting in Singapore to meet an old friend from Dubai!*

I was fairly certain the Singaporean taxi driver didn't understand *carsick*, but the tummy-rubbing pantomime did the trick. Muttering incoherently, the testy driver brushed his maps and papers off the passenger seat and grabbed his mobile phone just as I plopped myself down next to him. Fastening my seat belt, I caught a fleeting glimpse of something—another cell phone?—before the driver roughly heel-kicked it under his seat.

"It's on Havelock Road," I told him as we left the airport precinct.

"Havelock. Yes, yes, I know."

On the whirlwind ride back from the sleek Singapore Changi Airport to the Riverside Hotel, I had to admit my latest gambit was not going well.

We agreed Singapore would be an acceptable meeting place. So where was he? Could I have missed his arriving flight? I thought I had seen them all come in, but did I miss one? I waited past midnight, sat on my cell phone all day. Was I still in the loop? Did someone intervene, unbeknownst to me? Were events now spinning out beyond my control?

At long last, it was beginning to dawn on me that I was probably in over my head, but my mind was pretty numb and my body too tired to even think about trying another tack. It was one in the morning.

The cabdriver was chatting unintelligibly on his mobile phone as he slammed on the brakes at the Riverside entrance. I eased myself out the door, holding out cash as the driver reached for it with his free hand. The driver made an affected move in the direction of his change purse, but I held up my palm to indicate, "Keep the change." The driver nodded, feigned a half smile of appreciation, and continued jabbering on the phone.

Clutching my briefcase, this bone-weary rabbi breezed through the lobby to the unmanned front desk. I leaned over it in the vain hope of discovering a message in my pigeonhole, then headed out back toward the River Garden Coffee House.

Linda and I had stayed at the hotel before, and I knew the River Garden would be open well into the wee hours of the morning. Wallowing in frustration, I yearned to fill the void with food and drink, perhaps in some mindless conversation with a dispassionate stranger.

Nevertheless, I was somewhat wary when my eyes first fell upon her. She was seated at a table at the far corner of the parquet floor, near the delimiting bushes at the river's edge. It was a careful distance from the filtered light spilling through the lobby's large louvered windows into the outdoor café. As far as I could tell, she was the only other patron at that late hour.

She smiled at me as I settled into my chair at a table within earshot. She continued to stare. I looked behind me to see if her gaze was intended for someone else. When it became obvious the coast was clearly clear, I spoke up.

"Mind if I join you?" I asked, emboldened by her attention. What did I have to lose?

"Not at all," she said.

Linda's death was now far enough in the past that I could finally say without guilt that her passing was, in some ways, liberating. I mourned for her a full month and moped around a while after that. But before long, it was as if a whole new chapter opened up for me.

"I am Jon," I said confidently, offering my hand while seating myself to her side.

"My name is Laila," she said softly, looking about prudently before offering her hand in return.

At another time, in another place, I might have responded with, "Laila. How lovely. It means 'night' in Hebrew. Did you know that?" But I was cautious. I couldn't chance revealing too much of myself—not here, not now, not the fact I was a Hebrew speaker, let alone a rabbi. And I certainly didn't want to breathe a word of my reason for being here.

"Where are you from?" I asked.

"Male," she answered in a soft, silken voice, "capital of the Maldives. Do you know where that is?"

I did. *Ah, the Maldives,* I thought, smiling to myself. The travel brochures made the Maldives look so exquisite out there in the middle of the Indian Ocean, with powder-soft beaches and overwater bungalows built on stilts. "Tiki huts," the brochures called them, with their glass-floor cutouts unveiling a rainbow of sea life gliding below in azure-tinted lagoon waters.

We often thought about visiting the Maldives, but Linda refused to spend that many hours in an airplane for only a few days of vacation. Flying used to be so glamorous; over the years, it had become just an inconvenience. Plus, the Maldivian tourist season came at my busiest time, and I could never get away long enough. Perhaps now, on the verge of retirement, I could begin to plan a trip. If only I could find the right companion.

"Would you like another drink?" I asked, glancing at her nearly empty wineglass.

"No, thank you," she said.

I rose from the table to bring my own drink—a tall gin and tonic with a twist of lime—over from the bar.

"The Boxing Day tsunami woke us up to the fact that our island nation is sinking," she continued upon my return. "My island, for example, the main island, is only two meters above sea level. We know we must urgently begin to dredge the ocean floor and elevate our land before the next tsunami comes."

"And you've come to Singapore, why?"

"To find investors for that effort. We are Indian Maldivians, and Singapore has a strong—and notably generous—Indian community. We have found that if we can reach our Indian sisters, they will speak to their husbands. That's my job. To appeal to the women." She was looking directly at me now.

I glanced at the rings on her hand. "Are you married?"

"No," she said somberly. "My husband was one of the eighty-two Maldivians who died in the tsunami. That's why this cause is so important to me."

Though her words were tragic, I liked the way she seemed to swallow them, speaking from the back of her throat.

"I'm a widower myself," I offered, choking on a word I had never uttered before. It sounded pathetic, almost effeminate. My eyes began to moisten as Linda's tragic accident surged through my mind.

She looked around again, then took my hand in hers. "So we are both, shall we say, autonomous?"

"Yes," I said almost breathlessly.

This was too good to be true. A dark-haired, dark-eyed beauty alone in the River Garden. The perfect antidote for my abject frustration at the end of an abundance of days, many thousands of traveled miles, heightened anxiety, and not an insignificant amount of fear.

Her fingers were long, delicate. "Such strong hands," she said as she pulled my hand closer to her chest and began to examine my palm.

Her other hand dipped beneath the table edge as I began to respond to her advances, gazing intently into her dark-brown eyes, scrutinizing her olive-skinned face with approving glances.

Suddenly, her eyes turned cold. She clamped down on my hand, holding the palm tightly against the tabletop.

Oh, she likes it rough, was my first fleeting thought. But then I felt a sharp sting on a protruding vein.

It was the last thing I would feel. I did not see the needle as she jabbed it into me, so absorbed was I in the abrupt change in her visage.

Will I come out of this? I now wondered, struggling to seize hold of a single unraveling thread of consciousness.

As I began to drift off, my mind tumbled back through a lifetime of memories to the time and place where this whole improbable journey began.

CHAPTER II.

 MINNEAPOLIS. JUNE 1967.

Every matter in its proper time.
ECCLESIASTES 8:6

When I awoke on Monday, June 5, 1967, I was a baby boom-er college student with a great summer job. My employer was the Chicago Great Western Railroad, the CGW. Its branch headquarters was a quaint red cottage out in the middle of the rail yards where Minneapolis meets Saint Paul.

Luckily for me, the University of Michigan, where I attended as an out-of-state undergraduate, was on the trimester system, while the "other U of M," the University of Minnesota, operated on the quarter system. This enabled me to finish my studies in early May, come home to Minneapolis, and get a head start in the summer job market while the University of Minnesota was still in session.

The summer of '67 gave rise to a number of crosscurrents that helped define an entire generation. Like millions of middle-class college students that summer, I needed desperately to stay in school. The chilling background noise was provided by our gener-ation's war—Vietnam, a black hole lurking at the edge of our con-sciousness, threatening to suck us into its grisly vortex the moment our student deferments ran out. In sharp contrast, San Francisco's Haight-Ashbury neighborhood advertised a peaceable "love-in" that summer, drawing as many as a hundred thousand young people from all parts of the country. All the while, a number of inner-city neighborhoods simmered with racial tension. Within a few weeks, Newark, Cincinnati, Detroit, and even my own neighborhood—the old North Side of Minneapolis, once a largely Jewish neighborhood that was now more than 50 percent African American—would explode in urban violence. The "Summer of Love" transformed, for many, at least, into the "Long, Hot Summer."

I was filled with dread as I drove to my job that Monday morning, but not because of the turmoil in Vietnam or the inner-city ghetto violence. Rather, that first weekend of June, as well as the whole previous month, my world was disquieted by demoralizing fear of an impending holocaust: the State of Israel, surrounded by enemies who refused to accept her, was about to be pounced upon by her adversaries. In one powerful stroke after another, Egypt, Jordan, and Syria had formed a military alliance, cut off Israel's shipping lanes, ordered United Nations peacekeepers out of the Gaza Strip buffer zone, and moved troops within earshot of Tel Aviv and Jerusalem. It was not at all clear that Israel would survive the coming onslaught. News broadcasts from Tel Aviv showed dozens of young Israeli high schoolers digging graves, while thousands of soldiers moved to the front.

With a great deal of apprehension, I pulled into my assigned parking space outside the station office that Monday morning and tuned in to WCCO radio, the local CBS affiliate. What I heard next would reshape my entire world and provide me with a blueprint for the rest of my life.

"Good morning, everybody," the broadcast began. "This is Douglas Edwards and the news. This morning, Israeli aircraft launched a surprise attack against the air forces of Egypt, Syria, Jordan, and Iraq. Within two hours, the Israeli Air Force destroyed more than four hundred Arab aircraft on the ground. Israeli ground forces have begun moving into the Gaza Strip, driving back the Egyptian Army, which occupied the Strip after President Nasser ordered UN peacekeepers out. A few moments ago, they captured the Egyptian commander of Gaza, Major Mohammed Tamil. We have unconfirmed reports that Egyptian soldiers have abandoned their positions and are fleeing on foot into the Sinai desert."

The following Monday, when the dust had settled, I confidently knocked on the glass-paneled office door of the CGW stationmaster, D. F. Durling. The stationmaster sat in his wooden swivel chair behind a massive desk. He was an imposing figure, fully six foot three and a hefty 220 pounds or more. He wore brown suspenders over his immaculate white shirt, sported a red-and-brown-striped tie, and puffed mindlessly on a Dunhill Bruyere pipe while perusing some important documents. He was the very picture of a railroad stationmaster, from the cut of his hair to the dark-brown shirt garters.

"Come in and sit down, Jonathan," he bellowed but not altogether unkindly.

I strode in and sat down. There followed a brief uncomfortable silence.

"Chief"—I leaned forward a bit as I spoke to him—"I guess you've heard the news about Israel."

"Yeah, Jonathan. You guys really whupped 'em." There was a note of admiration in his words.

"Chief, I'd like to go help out over there—just for a couple of weeks—and then I'd like to come back to my job here," I boldly told him, finding new confidence in the remarkable turn of world events.

I needed the railroad job to help pay for the coming year's out-of-state college tuition, but at the same time, I wanted desperately to participate in this great moment in history.

Durling puffed on his pipe a few times, releasing a pleasant aroma of cherry and spice as he contemplated my request. When he was ready with his answer, he pulled the pipe out of his mouth, turned the stem toward the young switching clerk seated humbly at his desk, and poked the air between us as he spoke firmly.

"Son, we're satisfied with your work here, but the answer is no, you can't leave and come back."

"Okay. Thank you, Chief. Much obliged for your time," I managed to reply as I sheepishly slipped out of the chair and hustled back to my desk, my newfound self-confidence now knocked back a couple of pegs.

I was, after all, a nineteen-year-old, wet-behind-the-ears college sophomore in need of guidance. The stationmaster's answer that day would prove to be providential, though I didn't quite appreciate it at that time.

A month later, violence struck much nearer to home.

"I wouldn't go out on Plymouth Avenue tomorrow, Mrs. Kadison," warned our family's African American housekeeper, Celestine, a day before riots broke out on the old North Side.

By the next evening, Plymouth Avenue, the commercial lifeline of our community, looked like a war zone. Its shops were looted and burned; the avenue, its alleyways, and side streets were littered with glass and bricks. On the third day of rioting, the governor of Minnesota landed his helicopter at Sumner Field Park in a dramatic effort to quell the violence. It worked.

During my afternoon coffee break the same day, one railroad employee offered, "If you want my opinion, the cops ought to get in there with M16s and kill 'em all."

"No need for that," I offered in a gallant attempt to mollify the harsh rhetoric. "They're already shooting themselves in the foot. When it's all over, where are they gonna buy a loaf of bread? The stores are in shambles."

My beloved neighborhood was disintegrating. It was an unnerving time, but all I could do about it was avoid Plymouth Avenue and make sure our doors were double-locked. My parents soon began looking for a new home, finding one just over the city limits, and got ready to move before winter.

So went the summer of '67, the "Summer of Love" that had turned into the "Long, Hot Summer" while the Vietnam War raged on, the summer of Israel's stunning victory in the Six-Day War.

Jews came out of the woodwork that summer: Jews who had hardly identified as Jews; hidden Jews; secret Jews; Catholic descendants of Spanish Inquisition Jews, some of whom lit candles on Friday nights but didn't know why. They all came out that summer to celebrate Israel's surprise victory and claim their role in that historic drama.

My focus too had now shifted to the Middle East. I was determined to get over there as soon as I could. Staying on the job at CGW had made all the difference, as it turned out, as I was able to put in plenty of overtime. By the end of the summer, I had saved enough not only to pay for my final years of college but also for a student ticket to Tel Aviv. I arrived in the Holy Land two days after classes ended in May 1968.

CHAPTER III.

 THE SECOND MILLENNIUM CE.

Chi sta bene non si muove.
(Whoever has it good doesn't move.)
ITALIAN PROVERB

When we change our locality we change our luck.
TALMUD

I was already well versed in Middle Eastern matters even before I ventured abroad for the first time in 1968. My father, Rabbi Louis Kadison, had lived in pre-state Palestine and could produce a British Mandatory Palestinian passport to prove it. As a student and later as a rabbi, I took great pleasure in that aspect of my father's life, especially during the occasional debate over the Israel-Palestine conflict, when I would proudly proclaim, "My father is a Palestinian." Though technically correct but politically hyperbolic, it was nonetheless effective in putting my opponents on their back feet.

I liked to point out too the fact that some Jewish families, never having left the Holy Land, could trace their roots in Israel back more than two thousand years. And in response to the charge that the Jews stole Palestine in 1948, my comeback was always, "And what gave Muslims the right to occupy *our* land back in the year 636 and build two mosques on our most sacred site, the Temple Mount?" To Westerners—especially Americans, who tend to dismiss things that happened just a few months earlier as "ancient history"—arguing about some thirteen-hundred-year-old event might seem quaint, at best. But I had learned that Middle Easterners never forget perceived wrongs, that they can become just as incensed over events of the seventh century as events of the past seven days. However far back my opponents wanted to go, my study of history had prepared me with an answer.

My father had been born into a rabbinic family that could boast of eleven consecutive generations of rabbis, and he, Louis, now represented the twelfth. My father, sensing I was more naturally inclined toward Judaic matters than my two older brothers, often expressed the hope that I would someday come to represent the thirteenth rabbinic generation.

The family actually claims an earlier ancestor, one Shem Tov Halevi. A noted scholar born in 1005 in Barcelona, Spain, he in turn called himself "Hayitzhari," claiming descent from Yitzhar, grandson of Levi, one of the patriarch Jacob's twelve sons, founder of the eponymous biblical tribe.

"Nonsense," my skeptical wife, Linda, would say. "All we hear about are 'noble lineage' and 'past life' people nowadays. Everyone claims to be a descendant—or the reincarnation—of a king or a queen or a count or a baroness or, at the very least, someone very important in the past. So let me ask you, whatever happened to all those poor serfs—don't they have any present-life incarnations? Why doesn't anybody claim descent from a dirt-poor peasant? Or a lady of the night instead of a knight of the realm?"

"Ah, but we *do* have at least one villain in the mix," I told her, "the infamous Koraḥ, who led a failed rebellion against Moses. Wouldn't that be like a Union soldier's family celebrating John Wilkes Booth as an ancestor? Why would we claim the notorious Koraḥ if there weren't some truth to the tale?"

Linda still had a point, of course. Genealogists and parapsychologists are doing quite well nowadays—some charlatans among them no doubt telling people what they want to hear. So Linda remained skeptical. She didn't give much credence to my story, and to tell you the truth, I didn't much believe it either.

And for the longest time, I didn't much care. But then along came this thing called DNA research. In the late 1990s, genetic scientists put out a call for all those Jewish males who claimed to be Cohanim, descendants of the priests who served in the ancient temple. They measured their Y chromosomes and compared them with other Jews and non-Jews, and guess what? They found that a significantly high proportion of those claiming to be Cohanim today *do* in fact have a distinct genetic marker. They named it Y-chromosomal Aaron or the Cohen modal haplotype (CMH) and traced it back some 3,300 years to the approximate time of the Exodus from Egypt, 106 generations to the very lifetime of the Levite Aaron, brother of Moses!

"You don't have to believe me," I told Linda. "Just check the scientific journal *Nature*, the one published on July 9, 1998."

I'm not a scientist, but some of my friends tell me the magazine is pretty highly regarded. I'm a Levite claiming descent from the same tribe, and when they did my DNA, they found a high degree of consistency. Incredible as it may sound, scientists say the chances of these DNA findings happening at random are less than one in ten thousand.

As the Kadison family saga recounts and Jewish history carefully documents, Israelites, even before the rise of Christianity, spread throughout the Roman Empire and to the East—to Persia and central Asia, to Spain and Portugal, and to England, France, and Germany. In the fifteenth century, many migrated to Poland, Ukraine, Belarus, Lithuania, and Latvia.

My own grandfather, in fact, was the rabbi of a small Lithuanian shtetl, a small village on the border of Poland, when the czar of Russia, Nicholas II, ordered all Jews into the interior of Russia at the beginning of the First World War. Even though most Jews had remained loyal to his Romanov ancestor during the struggle against Napoleon a hundred years earlier, Nicholas now believed that the subsequent century of czarist oppression had turned the Jews into potential antagonists. He feared they would become a fifth column, forming an alliance with Germany in its drive toward the Russian interior, so he moved the Jews eastward, away from the front, enabling him to exercise tighter control.

My dad was a youngster at the time; all he could remember of that period was riding toward Moscow on the roof of a crowded eastbound train. He explained that riding on top of the train through the long night presented a very urgent problem. Where could they relieve themselves? They couldn't step to the edge of the car for fear of slipping off. Instead, they stood over the passenger-car vent shafts and did their business there.

"It was the only option we had short of soiling our own resting places," Louis Kadison recounted to his sons. Then with a measure of satisfaction in his voice, he added, "Besides, it gave us great pleasure to get back at those tough guys who pushed us aside to grab the inside seats. I'll never forget the chaos at that train station."

The family would end up spending the years of the Russian Revolution in turbulent Moscow, while young Louis was sent away to one of the few yeshiva boarding schools the new Bolshevik masters allowed to stay open.

During those tumultuous times, millions of young Russian Jews were caught up in the new currents of Enlightenment, Humanism, and Socialism—intellectual movements that dethroned traditional religion. They embraced a kind of secular religion that had moved eastward from Europe to find fertile soil in Russia. These intellectual currents swept the Old World away, and they did not stop flowing at the yeshiva's gate—despite the yeshiva administrators' vain attempts to hold them back. Darwin's book, *On the Origin of Species*, for example—a work that appeared to undermine the entire biblical account of Creation—was widely studied in those days, as were such disparate writers as Karl Marx and Charles Dickens, among others. Although such works were verboten on the yeshiva's premises, curious young minds could not be kept away from them. To illustrate the clash between the two worlds as he experienced it, Louis told his family:

> One morning I was walking along with a fellow student who tried to take in as much of a romance novel as he could between classes. He was completely engrossed in that forbidden book. As we were walking along the pathway from one building to the next, who was to approach us from the other direction but the headmaster himself! Were my friend to be caught reading a secular book would have meant certain expulsion for him. So I nudged him, warning him of the headmaster's approach,

and my quick-thinking friend, without missing a
beat, let the book drop to the sidewalk. He stopped,
picked it up, kissed it, and continued to read as the
headmaster passed by.

The gesture, as we Kadison boys well knew, was intended to indicate to the headmaster that the book he was reading was a holy
book. The school administrator was none the wiser for the clever
gambit.

During the revolution, Louis's father once noted that many of
the Bolshevik leaders had Jewish surnames. He asked his worldlier
son, "Are these Communists in fact Jews?"

"Yes, Tatti. Many of them are. Trotsky, for example," Louis
reportedly replied.

"And are they regular shul-goers?" his father inquired.

"No, Tatti, they are not—not in the least. I doubt that any of
them have stepped inside a synagogue since their Bar Mitzvahs."

"That's not possible," replied the father in an incredulous tone.
"Do you mean to tell me they don't even go to shul on Rosh Hashanah and Yom Kippur?"

Louis's father—absorbed throughout his life in the cloistered
domain of rabbinic law and totally immersed for much of his life
in the affairs of a tiny eastern European shtetl—could not comprehend a world in which there were Jews who would not attend
synagogue on the High Holy Days.

Louis's mother, on the other hand—a worldly, university-ed-
ucated woman—eked out a modest living teaching English and
French in Moscow while her rabbi husband studied and taught
Torah. Soon they came to realize they would have to leave the
growing antibourgeois and antireligious climate of postrevolution

Russia before they became trapped forever in the Communist system. The Soviets were only too happy to let people out in those early years before the Iron Curtain descended; to them, it meant fewer mouths to feed. But the emigrants would have to leave everything behind.

"It was a case of push-pull. We felt pushed out of Russia because we weren't Communists and at the same time pulled toward the hope of building a Jewish home in Palestine," Louis explained to his children.

Just before they departed for Palestine, his mother sewed several Russian rubles into the lining of her fur coat. With that money, she bought land along the Yarkon River, the northernmost boundary of the new Jewish city of Tel Aviv, certain that the property would increase in value as the city grew.

Louis Kadison, a bright student of Talmud, entered a Jerusalem seminary and quickly obtained his ordination. Seeing as British Mandate Palestine was already flooded with immigrant rabbis, he headed for America, where, with a student visa in hand, he enrolled in the Hebrew Theological College in Chicago, Illinois, eager to obtain his American ordination. Along the way, he acquired a master's degree in social work.

Louis took student pulpits in Omaha, Nebraska, and Green Bay, Wisconsin, before settling in Cleveland, Ohio, where he met his wife, Rachel, and raised two boys.

Rachel Rubin was born in Cleveland, but her parents were Lithuanian Jewish immigrants. Her father, Meyer, had an especially captivating immigration story. Meyer had been forced into the czar's army in 1895 and sent to a boot camp not far from his hometown. Meyer's father, a peddler with considerable carpentry skills, traded with the base, among other customers, and had helped build its wooden barracks.

Shortly after Meyer reported to the training camp, his father built a small compartment within his horse-drawn wagon—a space with room enough for one person to lie flat. He then loaded the wagon with leeches, confident that border guards and tax authorities would avoid inspecting this particular load too carefully. He drove up to the army base, his son hopped the fence, and he secreted Meyer within the specially made compartment. He then drove his leech-filled wagon all day and all night to the Polish port of Gdańsk, where a steamer bound for America was due to set sail. Meyer never looked back.

In 1946, my father was called to the pulpit of Tiferes Israel synagogue in Minneapolis, and I, Jonathan Jacob, their third son, was born two years later. My mother became quite well known for her beautiful liturgical poetry, which Louis and, later, I would often incorporate into our Sabbath and holiday services—along with dozens of American rabbis.

Upon their arrival in Minneapolis, the family settled on the old North Side, a bustling neighborhood where the Jewish community made up an entire world for the Kadisons. Some of our neighbors were rabbis and cantors and Hebrew school teachers, but my education came from a variety of sources.

In one memorable incident, in fact, I'm not afraid to say my spiritual mentor appeared in the form of an elementary school classmate named Victoria Gunderson.

CHAPTER IV.

 MINNEAPOLIS. DECEMBER 1958.

Who is wise? The one who learns from everyone.
PIRKEI AVOT: SAYINGS OF THE FATHERS, CHAPTER IV

I might say the seed of my spiritual awakening was sown on Flag Day, June 14, 1954, when President Dwight David Eisenhower signed into law a joint resolution of Congress that added two reverential new words, "under God," to the Pledge of Allegiance. When American students would return to their classrooms the following September, the president proclaimed upon affixing his signature to the resolution, they were now required to rise each morning to face their classroom flag, place their right hands over their hearts, and recite in unison the Pledge of Allegiance, but henceforth and forevermore, they were to insert the two new words into the recitation.

By the time we entered the fifth grade in 1958, therefore, my classmates and I were already well versed in pledge protocol. But the teacher of that fifth-and-sixth-grade combined class, Mrs. Mabel Barabee, had some singular didactic notions. She was, as would soon become readily apparent, a zealot for grammar. So on the very first school day, following the recitation of the pledge, she made her way briskly to the blackboard and scribed the entire text on the board for the combined class to analyze:

I pledge allegiance to the Flag of the United States of America, and to the Republic for which it stands, one Nation under God, indivisible, with liberty and justice for all.

"You see," said the schoolmarm in her stern pedagogic tone, "the phrase is written thusly: 'one Nation under God.' There is no comma—that is, no separation between the words 'one Nation' and 'under God.' We are a nation under God and cannot be separated from Him. Therefore, from now on, in this classroom, and I daresay for the rest of your lives, you will recite it as one fluid phrase: 'one Nation under God.' There is to be no pause within that phrase. It is *not* 'one Nation, under God,'" she continued to expound, her voice now rising to a fever pitch, "but rather 'one Nation under God.' It is one meaningful phrase—a single, unitary statement—even though most Americans break it up into two. *They* are saying it wrong. *We will say it correctly!* Now, shall we practice?"

Of course, none of us children quite understood our dear teacher's punctuational reprimand nor the meaning of the absence of the pause within the phrase, and if the truth were told, we are still puzzled by it to this day. And although the word of the classroom teacher was the word of law, especially in the 1950s, habits are hard to break. Inevitably in those first few months of the school year, one or another of the boys—it was almost always a boy—would reinsert the pause and fall out of sync with the rest of the class. Consequently, any early-morning visitor to that classroom during those autumn months would have witnessed the entire class dutifully standing, placing hands over hearts, directing their obedient eyes toward the flag, and reciting the pledge in nearly perfect unison, which sounded something like this:

> *I pledge allegiance to the Flag of the United States of America, and to the Republic for which it stands, one Nation under God—der God, indivisible—sible, with liberty—erty and justice—tice for all—fr'all.*

The instant that first echo was heard, students would strain to keep their faces turned toward the flag as their eyes darted from side to side, sweeping the classroom as best they could to quickly pinpoint the perpetrator of the pledge-pause crime, the one who had fallen out of sync with his classmates. As for the perpetrator, so ensconced would he be in his blissful bubble of oblivion that only at the last moment, with that final slurred syllable hanging in the air for all to hear, would he become aware of his misdeed. He'd sheepishly sink back into his seat—his furtive, head-down glances met by headshakes of disgust from the girls and deceitful grins from his male classmates. For the rest of the day, he would become the butt of some of the unkindest kind of preadolescent teasing. He—again, it was almost always a "he"—would become the stooge, the dimwit, the classroom dunce of the day, all with Mrs. Barabee's tacit approval.

But on the last day of the first term, just before what used to be called "Christmas vacation," as my eyes began to sweep the room in search of that day's dunce, they alighted upon a phenomenon that shook me to my very core. So much so that I risked evoking Mrs. Barabee's dreadful scorn as I turned my face completely away from the flag in a rapid double take to behold the spectacle in its entirety.

There—standing in the very last row of the classroom, carefully placed at the back to prevent precisely the discovery that was now taking place—stood sixth-grader Victoria Gunderson. To my amazement, the bespectacled Victoria was standing, to be sure, but she stood with her arms held rigidly at her sides, her eyes were affixed to the blackboard straight ahead, and her lips were not moving! In the midst of the recitation of the Pledge of Allegiance, she was the only person in the room not reciting the pledge!

As we began to slink noisily back into our seats, I called across the room to my buddy James Waldorsky, who made it his business to know everybody's business and would, most fittingly, grow up to become a gossip columnist for the *Moose Lake Herald-Tribune*.

"James," I called out. But when I realized all eyes were now on *me*, I sank down into my chair and whispered in Waldorsky's direction, "Talk to you later."

I could hardly hold still before morning recess to dig up the dirt on Victoria Gunderson. As we all headed out the playground doors for recess, I ran up behind my friend James, grabbed his shoulder, and, turning him sideways, chattered excitedly to him in a hushed voice.

"Jimmy! Jimmy! What's with Vicky? Is she a Communist or something? She doesn't say the pledge. Did you see that? Is she one of those *un-Americans?*"

I had once overheard my parents speak in hushed tones about some "McCarthy House" in Washington, where "un-American activities" happened—or something like that. I could not understand how anyone could refuse to say the pledge. My classmates and I—children of the generation that survived the Great Depression and won the Great War, *grand*children of penniless immigrants who had struggled their way up the economic ladder—would never dare to show such disrespect to the flag of the grandest nation on earth!

"No, dummy!" answered James Waldorsky in his customary condescending manner. "She's not a Communist. And she's not an 'un-American' either, you dolt. She's a Jehovah's Witness. They don't say the pledge. They don't sing the 'Star-Spangled Banner.' They don't even sing 'Happy Birthday'!"

"What?" I was incredulous. I was dumbfounded. Drawing upon my mother's favorite expression, I shook my head this way and that, muttering, "Why, I never heard of such a thing!" and made secret plans to torment Vicky on her way home.

I stared in her direction as often as I could that day, trying to discover any other unusual behavior I might use as ammunition against her. When the final bell rang, I dashed out the door and ran a few yards along the street toward Vicky's home. Not that I knew precisely where she lived; I was certain only that it was in the opposite direction from my home. Hiding behind a tree, I waited for her to come by.

When she did appear, I began to taunt her from my hideout in a loud singsong voice, "Vicky's a Communist—she doesn't say the pledge! Vicky's un-American—she doesn't say the pledge!"

"Come out from behind that tree, Jonathan Kadison!" roared Victoria Gunderson in a commanding tone. "I can see your footprints in the snow, and I know your voice."

I had made no plans beyond the taunting, fully expecting a mortified Vicky to hurry on by. But now, busted, as it were, I sheepishly moved out from behind the tree at her imperious command.

Staring at the ground, shuffling my feet a bit, and now suddenly at a loss for words, I muttered in a subdued whisper, "Uh . . . uh . . . uh . . . Merry Christmas, Vicky."

"Oh, *we* don't *celebrate* Christmas, Jonathan," she replied in an animated voice. "In that way, we're a lot like you, aren't we? You don't celebrate Christmas either, do you? Would you like to learn more about my religion? I can bring you a copy of the *Junior Watchtower* after the vacation. It's a great magazine, just for kids like us. If you like it, I can get you a subscription. Just give me your address."

"Uh . . . no thanks," I called back to her, as by that time I, now utterly humiliated, had begun to rush away in the opposite direction, toward my own neck of the woods. As she continued her enthusiastic, rapid-fire harangue, I picked up speed and broke into a gallop.

It was already 3:30 in the afternoon on Friday, the twelfth of December 1958, the sixth day of Hanukkah. I knew that in less than an hour, just before sunset, my family and I would be standing in front of the Hanukkah menorah, and it would be my turn to light the candles for the seventh night of the eight-night festival.

As I headed home, I began to reflect on the events of that final day of the first term in Mrs. Barabee's class. I considered how my furtive glance had, purely by accident, come to rest upon the stalwart Victoria Gunderson, surrounded by her thirty classmates yet totally alone, holding her ground against a classroom full of conformists, standing up for her beliefs—a minority of one. She was certainly a resilient person, that Vicky Gunderson, as I would ultimately come to appreciate.

That evening as I stood with my family before the menorah, a lesson from another teacher rang in my ears.

"Up to this point, you've all learned that Hanukkah is about the miracle of the oil lasting for eight days," my Hebrew teacher, the ever-popular Mr. Michael King, began. "But now you are old enough to learn that that is not the real story of Hanukkah. The real story of Hanukkah is about a very small band of Judeans who stood up for the right to practice Judaism as they saw fit. It was a rebellion against Antiochus IV's attempt to force everyone to conform to his religion, the pagan Greek way. Most of Judea had been willing to go along with Antiochus. But this small band, the Maccabees, struggling to hold their ground against a sea of conformity, took it upon themselves to fight for the freedom to worship God in their own way. It was, in fact, the first battle for religious freedom the world has ever known. That freedom is now guaranteed by the First Amendment to the Constitution of the United States of America."

Mr. King's words, "struggling to hold their ground against a sea of conformity," now awakened my budding Jewish pride. I thought about my confrontation with Vicky Gunderson earlier that day, wondering where she had found the spiritual strength to withstand the pressure, how she had stood up for her beliefs, so straight and so resolute, while everyone else was headed in a different direction.

Over time, I would come to admire Vicky Gunderson's fortitude and strive to emulate her strength of character. She was like a shoe that didn't quite fit, but the social isolation didn't seem to faze her. Over time, I would come to appreciate that on that day in December 1958, I had encountered a modern-day Maccabee, and her name was Victoria Gunderson.

CHAPTER V.

 TEL AVIV. MAY 1968.

I will gather you from among the nations and bring you back from the countries where you were scattered.

EZEKIEL 11:17

On my first full day in Israel a decade later, my Tel Aviv cousin Ilana took me out in her car to a vast, open field before the Hills of Ephraim, a few miles east of the city. It was May 14, 1968, Israel's twentieth birthday.

"Do you see the rocks strewn all about, Yonatan?" She called me by my Hebrew name, meaning "God has given." "These rocks and boulders represent the burdens we Jews have carried on our shoulders for more than two thousand years—twenty long centuries of running from pillar to post, seeking a safe haven." Ilana narrated like a tour guide as her hand glided over the landscape before us.

I thought about the events of the "Long, Hot Summer" of '67 and reflected upon the fact that in the Minneapolis riots the majority of the shops—the gas stations, the grocery stores, the pharmacies, the barbershops, the delis, even the bowling alley—nearly all the ruined businesses were Jewish owned. No one could deny a strong element of anti-Semitism in the violence, though the media, perhaps not wishing to make a bad situation even worse, kept that fact out of circulation, portraying it as black versus white, poor against middle class. Nevertheless, in a neighborhood that was once home to more than twenty-one thousand Jews, there remained fewer than a thousand by the following summer. They'd all fled to the suburbs, including my own family.

"When our people arrive here safe in their homeland at last," my sabra cousin continued as if speaking to a larger audience, "their burdens roll off their backs. That's what these rocks represent. With this terrible weight off our shoulders, we are able to stand straighter and prouder and become masters of our own destiny."

Ilana's story touched my heart, I must admit. Her words brought the entire past year into sharp focus. She was a striking, raven-haired beauty; a no-nonsense young law student; an only child, five years my senior, who had traveled the world with her diplomat parents.

Her father, a seventh-generation Jerusalemite, was dispatched to Switzerland during World War II to participate in the desperate effort to bring Jewish refugees as immigrants to Palestine in defiance of British Mandatory restrictions. Later, he represented the new State of Israel in Cape Town, South Africa, and Ottawa, Canada, as part of its nascent diplomatic corps. In 1965, he became assistant attorney general for the State of Israel, his highest posting, while Ilana's mother, my father's sister, lectured in the English Department of the Hebrew University.

Ilana, like her parents, spoke English with a carefully cultivated British accent; it somehow made her words sound more authoritative to my casual midwestern ears. They had lived all over

31

the world but made it clear to everyone that Israel was their home. She was telling me it could be mine as well.

Two days later, at her suggestion, I boarded a train to Jerusalem, intent on finding my way to the Western Wall, Judaism's holiest site and last remnant of the ancient Temple. When Muslims conquered Jerusalem in 636 CE, they built two mosques upon the Temple ruins, while Jews continued to pray—as they do to this day—at the base of the western retaining wall, the Western Wall, also known as the Wailing Wall.

When I disembarked at the central train station, I marched the mile distance without a map, drawn as if by some magnetic attraction, straight to the Wall. There I heaved a weighty sigh, as Ilana's story of the rock-burdens seemed to manifest itself in my own body. Taking out the pen and paper I had brought with me for the occasion, I wrote down a brief poem to insert into a crack in the Wall:

> *Israel, here I reach your summit.*
> *And you are now, forever,*
> *My spiritual home,*
> *My temporal haunt,*
> *My rock-strewn palace.*

This was it. I had, at long last, arrived at a principal milestone on my life's journey. In a minor but not insignificant way, I had carried within me the weight of history, and the struggle had taken its toll.

I was, after all, one of "you guys" to my stationmaster, an outsider in certain circles, a member of a minority group desperately trying to secure its place in mainstream America. Somewhat like my classmate Victoria Gunderson, I felt a bit like a shoe that didn't quite fit.

Except here, in the Israel of 1968, here I somehow felt at home. Here that heavy burden rolled off my shoulders, and as a consequence, I could stand a little straighter here. Something beyond words was at work in that land.

CHAPTER VI.

 JERUSALEM. JUNE 1968.

A man of God appeared to me.

JUDGES 13:6

Among my prominent relatives was the esteemed Nazir of Jerusalem, Rabbi Gabriel Kadison. As a young student at the University of Basel, Switzerland, Gabriel had been well on his way to an academic career in philosophy during the First World War. Then he met the chief rabbi of Palestine, a mystic named Abraham Isaac Kook, who had come to the university as a guest lecturer.

The saintly Rabbi Kook, a pious leader who was nevertheless known to dance in Jerusalem's public square with young atheist Jewish farmers, held that the growing Zionist movement was a harbinger of a Messianic Age. Despite the fact that the new movement was composed chiefly of secular Jews who believed in a humanistic "religion of labor" rather than a supernatural God, he was adored by these young secular Jews, who saw in him the melding of their grandparents' religion and their new worldly philosophy.

Under Rabbi Kook's spiritual guidance, the intense young student Gabriel immersed himself in the study of Kabbalah in a further attempt to comprehend the true nature of the universe. He later took upon himself the rare Nazirite vow based on a passage from the Book of Numbers, an oath that included abstention from meat, from wearing leather, from cutting his hair, and from partaking of any products of the vine. Gabriel Kadison's self-discipline went even further; it also encompassed frequent self-imposed silences and a vegan diet decades before it became fashionable. In addition, he swore to speak the sacred tongue, Hebrew, only on the holy Sabbath and not on any other day. He also vowed, once he arrived in the Holy Land, never to leave the sacred city of Jerusalem.

He was, however, anything but a hermit. For example, he married his childhood sweetheart; fathered two children, a boy and a girl; and remained vitally involved in the life of Jerusalem. In fact, the day after Israel conquered Jerusalem in 1967, even before all pockets of resistance had been eliminated, Gabriel Kadison, the Nazir of Jerusalem, famously promenaded through the newly captured Old City, escorted by his son-in-law, chief chaplain of the Israel Defense Forces (IDF), as they made their way to the Western Wall.

When I approached the Nazir's house, his diminutive wife, Shayna Bluma, met me at the door. Shayna Bluma had fallen in love with Gabriel well before he came under the spell of Chief Rabbi Kook. They had been students together in Basel—secular, socialist, Zionist idealists. Shayna Bluma, who majored in agronomy, dreamed of going up to the land of Israel to become part of a kibbutz. Religion was far from her mind, but Gabriel was close to her heart, so consequently—perhaps somewhat reluctantly, although she never publicly betrayed a note of regret—she chose to follow him.

I came to their door expecting to meet the Nazir straight away, but Shayna Bluma led me instead into her kitchen at the rear of their small stone house in Jerusalem's crowded Meah Shearim neighborhood. Gesturing toward the large window over her kitchen sink, she indicated a small backyard with a well-tended garden.

"You see," she said with an ironic smile, "this is my kibbutz."

Next she brought me into the Nazir's study. There I beheld the Nazir himself, now in his midseventies, small in stature but sturdily built. He looked like a lion, with a wide, mangy white beard encircling his face. His reddish hair, tinged with yellow-white streaks, piled up in braids behind his ears and over his back and shoulders. He had lively blue eyes and wore a burgundy caftan trimmed with golden thread and a white silken scarf, under which he tucked whatever he could of his long reddish hair. On his head sat a large white satin pillbox-shaped skullcap similarly with gold piping.

The Nazir sat at one end of a long rough-hewn wooden table. A dozen chairs were scattered here and about. All four walls were lined with heavily laden floor-to-ceiling bookshelves, broken up on one side by a double-hung window and on another side by the doorway.

I was escorted to the far end of the table and seated next to the rabbi, while Shayna Bluma took her place at the opposite end near the doorway, watching the two cousins from such different worlds, listening to their interchange, and translating for them. I could speak some Hebrew, but this was a Tuesday, and I knew the rabbi spoke Hebrew only on the Sabbath. So I spoke English while Shayna Bluma translated my words into Yiddish for the Nazir, and vice versa.

Virtually everyone who came into the Nazir's study brought with him a serious question for the holy man to answer. I, for one, had been so moved by the events of June 1967 that they transformed my entire world outlook. I remembered how I had shuddered at the sight of Egyptian, Syrian, Jordanian, even Iraqi forces lining up on Israel's borders while cadres of Israeli teenagers dug graves in preparation for what was expected to come. And I still felt that unbridled pride from when Israel emerged victorious, when the whole world woke up to the fact that, this time, the people of Israel refused to submit and be slaughtered.

So I asked the Nazir, "Was the Six-Day War of cosmic significance?" Was Israel's stunning victory in that conflict more than a "mundane" matter of advanced weaponry, diligent training, and innovative tactics?

In other words, was there a divine dimension to this historic moment in world history?

When the question had been communicated, the rabbi nodded in understanding, as if he himself had considered the very same matter. A pensive expression fell over his face as he said something in Yiddish to Shayna Bluma across the room. She got up, looked about, reached up to a shelf slightly above her head, drew down a large dark-red bound volume off the shelf, and brought it to the Nazir.

As I pulled my chair a little closer to look at the text with him, the Nazir asked me to read. It was a text from the Talmudic volume Zevaḥim, written about a time when the Temple of Jerusalem still stood.

I was familiar with the form though not the content of the passage before me. "*B'aḥad sh'areḥa*," I read aloud from the bold print of the heading, then I continued on from the regular script, "*B'sha'ah shekol Yisrael niḥnasin b'shaar eḥad.*"

Looking about the page before me, I recognized that the Talmudic passage was based on a biblical text from the Book of Deuteronomy regarding the Passover offering. The translation: "In one of your gates: [The proper offering can be made on the altar of the Temple] only at the time when all Israel enters through a single gate."

The Nazir spoke a few sentences to Shayna Bluma, and she explained:

> Jerusalem, as you know, is the eternal capital of the Jewish people. It is both the subject of our prayers and the direction in which we pray. The Temple Mount in Jerusalem has always been the focal point of the entire Jewish people, wherever we are in the world. Had we captured only the Sinai Peninsula and the Golan Heights in last year's Six-Day War, we would still be cut off from our holiest site. It was only when we conquered Jerusalem's Old City that the war acquired "cosmic significance," as you put it.
>
> The text you read said that for the Almighty to be properly worshipped in Jerusalem, "All of Israel must enter through one gate." This rare phrase, written centuries ago, is especially prophetic in light of your question.

When she paused, the Nazir spoke again. I sensed that he understood English well enough but preferred to involve Shayna Bluma in the exchange. As she translated, the Nazir explained his sense of the passage:

During the War of Independence in 1948, our Haganah defense forces broke through Zion Gate at the southwest corner of the Old City, while the Irgun underground force tried, unsuccessfully, to break through Damascus Gate in the north. As you know, our son was wounded and captured along with dozens of others by the Jordanian legion in that battle.

At that time, we were in a state of internal discord, with the two distinct militias vying for control. There was no single command, no coordination, and no unity. As a consequence, we lost the battle for the Old City. Had we succeeded in conquering it then, though, quarrels would have broken out over which group had won the battle and who deserved to be in charge. Jerusalem would have become a cause for disunity and division.

But Jerusalem is the eternal capital of the entire Jewish people, not this group or that group. Like your Washington and other capital cities, it stood at the boundary between the tribes in a sort of no-man's-land, a city founded on concord and harmony. For this reason, it was only last year when our IDF—the army representing the entire nation of Israel and, by extension, Jewish people all over the world—poured in through a single gate, the Lion's Gate, securing our holy sites and unifying the entire city of Jerusalem once again. Only then did the Six-Day War reach its culmination and acquire a sacred dimension.

So, yes, indeed, the war was far more than a matter of weapons, tactics, or training. We drove our enemies back, but most important, we regained control of the Holy City for the first time in two thousand years. As your own American Rabbi Abraham Joshua Heschel has said, "History is not made by man alone." Our victory was sanctioned by a power even greater than a strong will to succeed, born out of desperation. The ultimate achievement of the war, the unification of Jerusalem, was spoken of many centuries ago. And now the Almighty has brought us, through this victory, one more important step closer to the Messianic Age.

The Nazir nodded and smiled at his wife, indicating that she had spoken well.

We continued to chat for a little while longer. They explained that twenty years earlier in the War of Independence, their son and the other war prisoners had been treated well under orders of King Abdullah, the Jordanian monarch, and later repatriated to Israel in a prisoner exchange.

Shayna Bluma smiled as she remarked, "Some people like to say that with enemies like Jordan, who needs friends?" We all chuckled at the heavy irony in her words. Then she said, "If peace ever comes to Israel, it will start with Jordan."

Sensing it was time to leave, I presented them with a small gift from my parents and shortly thereafter bade farewell to Shayna Bluma and the Nazir of Jerusalem.

A year later, the prime minister of Israel, Golda Meir, offered yet another explanation for Israel's victory in the Six-Day War. In the prime minister's residence, not far from the Nazir's home, the newly elected leader held a private meeting with visiting US senator Joe Biden.

As Senator Biden later recounted, he asked the prime minister how it had been possible for Israel to conquer enemies far more numerous and more abundantly equipped.

She told him, "Don't worry, Senator—we have a secret weapon."

As they stepped out of her office for the mandatory press photos, the prime minister could see the puzzled look on the senator's face. Was she alluding to Israel's often-denied-but-widely-assumed top secret nuclear capability?

But as the cameras clicked away, she whispered to him, "Our secret weapon is this: we have no other place to go. Our soldiers fight with their backs against the wall because we simply have no other place to go."

How *did* Israel manage to defeat its formidable enemies in June of 1967? Was it a matter of divine guidance, or the simple fact that, with no other place to go, its forces fought with extraordinary zeal? Was its victory a manifestation of the supernatural, or a product of this natural world? Perhaps the truth lies somewhere in between.

CHAPTER VII.

 JORDAN VALLEY. SUMMER 1968.

Your children shall return to their borders.

JEREMIAH 31:17

After the audience with the Nazir, my soul was on fire. I promised myself to see and learn everything I could about this dynamic young country before I returned to my studies. I was especially delighted that I had told my University of Michigan friend Phillip Reinfeld about my travel plans.

"I've got an uncle on a kibbutz up north," Phillip had said when I shared my travel itinerary with him.

"A kibbutz? I'd love to go there. Can you write to him for me?"

"Not a problem," Phillip offered. "And I'll have him write a letter of introduction for you to give to the kibbutz manager. He said I could come anytime, so you can be my representative for now, until I can make the trip myself."

When I told Ilana of the connection and showed her the letter, she became quite animated. "That's perfect, Yonatan," she said. "Go up to the Jordan Valley if you want to see the real Israel. Perhaps you can volunteer on his kibbutz. They're under fire now, and they need volunteers, so with your friend's letter, you have a good chance of being accepted."

Kibbutz Haziv, shaped like a gloved fist and perched above the road that runs along the Jordan River, was in the news that summer practically every other day, so the entire populace of Israel was well aware of its predicament. Its history was quite remarkable. In 1948, the Arab Legion—under the leadership of Sir Clive Lawrence-Cole, a British general with an affinity for the Arab point of view—attacked it, however unsuccessfully. Later in the War of Independence, the kibbutz withstood a second onslaught, this time from the Iraqi army. Now it was on the front line of still another war, as yet unnamed, which began shortly after the Six-Day War.

During those anxious six days of 1967, thousands of Arab refugees fled the violence by heading eastward over the Jordan River into the Hashemite Kingdom of Jordan. Among them were small bands of Palestinian fighters, members of Yasser Arafat's Palestine Liberation Organization. Within six months of the Six-Day War, they had set up positions in Jordan on the east bank of the Jordan River, creating havoc with Israel all along the border—from the Sea of Galilee in the north to the Dead Sea in the south. Kibbutz Haziv was, apparently, among their best-loved targets.

I did not think twice about entering this scene of the conflict. In fact, I relished it, confident the vaunted IDF would keep me safe. I only hoped my ability to converse in simple, everyday Hebrew would secure me a place on the kibbutz and enable me to experience what Ilana called "the real Israel."

So with a small backpack strapped over my shoulders, I boarded a bus bound from Jerusalem to Kibbutz Haziv. As we approached the Jordan River Valley and turned northward, a fellow passenger leaned over and spoke to me in broken English.

"Here this bus was attacked by a sniper last week, at the next stop. One of our neighbors was killed when he stepped out from the bus. So I advise you to move to this side of the bus when a seat becomes available. Keep your eyes open and your head down as we drive along the Jordan."

As the bus turned north onto Highway 90, I changed seats as advised. My wary eyes began to notice successive numbers stenciled onto each roadway culvert. The helpful passenger explained that the culverts served a dual purpose: to convey runoff from the hills, of course, and to serve as shelter in case of an outbreak of shelling from the Jordanian side, only a few hundred yards to the east. The numbers would pinpoint the precise location of each culvert, giving the IDF vital information in case of an attack.

As the bus picked up speed on the northward journey, army jeeps began to replace civilian cars on the road. It soon became apparent that this was, in fact, a war zone, but at the same time, a regular part of everyday life in Israel. They had gotten used to living under fire.

When the bus arrived at the kibbutz, I went straight to the office, where the manager, a burly lady named Teḥiah, presided.

"I'm a friend of Shimon Reinfeld," I said boldly, producing the letter of introduction from Phillip's uncle, whom I had yet to meet, "and I'd like to volunteer for a while, if I may."

She looked me over, perused the letter, conversed with me a bit in simple Hebrew, then gave me a blue canvas sack of clothing: three pairs of dark kibbutz shorts; four khaki shirts; and a blue *kova tembel*, a silly sort of conical cloth cap that did nothing to shield the sun from the wearer's eyes but covered the top of the head.

"When you want these work clothes washed, just put them in this bag and carry it over to the *maḥbesah*, the laundry. If you bring it before work in the morning, you'll have it back by dinnertime the same day."

I found my way to the volunteer dormitory, chose a single bed, then went out to find Shimon Reinfeld.

Everyone knows everyone on an Israeli kibbutz, even on the large ones with more than fifteen hundred residents. Kibbutz Haziv had only 650 members, so I easily discovered the way to Shimon's place: a three-room, one-story row house, austerely furnished, with a small patio in front. The home had a bathroom, a bedroom, and a living room, where a half wall separated a kitchenette in a corner. Every house was the same, so it was pretty much that way on all 230 kibbutzim throughout Israel.

Shimon was a soft-spoken mustachioed German immigrant who had arrived after Kristallnacht—the Night of the Broken Glass—in 1938. He married a "daughter of the kibbutz" named Dafna, and they had two teenaged boys and a girl, his firstborn, who was now in the army. None of the children lived at home; at age fourteen, kibbutz children moved to a special area set aside for them during their high school years. It was something like going off to summer camp and sharing a bunk with three or four others, only this situation prevailed year-round. As Shimon described it to me that first day, the system gave the teenagers all the independence they craved at that particular period in their lives. They would visit their parents' house for tea at 4:00 each day and, on most occasions, join them for dinner in the communal dining room at 7:00. All meals for all residents—breakfast, lunch, and dinner—were taken in the communal dining room, the social center of the kibbutz.

Shimon managed the farm machinery shop for the community. In the small patio in front of his house, he had built a metal sculpture garden out of shrapnel from mortars and artillery shells that had landed in the kibbutz. Some of it bore Arabic, some Russian, and some English markings. Around his neck, he wore an unfired Uzi machine gun bullet, devoid of gunpowder, with a hole drilled through the casing for the chain to pass through. It was a kind of necklace worn by younger men—and some older ones too—throughout Israel.

"Do you like it?" Shimon inquired.

"Very much," I genuinely replied.

"I can make you one tomorrow if you come by my shop after work."

I still wear that chain made for me by Shimon Reinfeld in 1968.

At dinner in the communal dining hall a few hours later, Yoav, the volunteer coordinator, came over to me.

"Tomorrow at 7:00, you will help dig the trenches. Shimon's son here will show you what to do, then he'll go to class."

Early the next morning, I was awoken by the sound of a backhoe in the distance. It was digging a trench roughly four feet wide and six feet deep, extending from the bomb shelter doorway toward the four-building courtyard that included my volunteer dormitory.

I was shown how to place corrugated metal sheets along both sides of the trench and then set in U-shaped steel struts eight feet apart to hold the metal sheets in place.

Virtually every night after farmers and workers on both sides of the Jordan River had completed their work, gunshots would emanate from the east. Kibbutzniks knew to run along the trench toward the doorway of the shelter whenever the gunfire escalated into more deadly, long-range mortar fire. To enter the shelter, ironically, they would have to come back up to the surface momentarily because the thick-concrete bunker-like entrance stood above ground. The entrance then sloped abruptly downward, forming the roof of an enclosed stairway that enabled the kibbutzniks to move quickly to the shelter's elaborate set of underground rooms.

Every night, it was the same: single rifle shots along the river bank, an occasional machine gun burst, followed by larger explosions—then, more often than not, quiet.

But one night I clearly remember to this day, the sounds got louder, more persistent, and frighteningly closer to the kibbutz residential area. Then suddenly, a deafening *boom* and *whoosh* were heard as an artillery shell landed about fifty yards away, throwing up shrapnel and grass and soil and gravel, which then plummeted to the ground. It was followed by another salvo, then another. After the second shell landed too close for comfort, half-dressed kibbutzniks, myself included, could be seen scurrying out along the grass in the dark, silhouetted by walkway lamps, ducking into the unfinished trenches, shuffling along to the shelter entrance, while still others stayed above ground the whole distance.

After about an hour in the shelter, one of the IDF soldiers stationed on the kibbutz announced the all clear, shouting down from the doorway. The kibbutz residents went back to bed. In the morning, the damage would be surveyed and repaired immediately.

Normally, Friday in Israel is a four-hour workday, as residents throughout the land leave work early to prepare for the Jewish Sabbath, which begins at sunset. In the early afternoon, men dressed in dark pants and white shirts can be seen throughout the land with bouquets of flowers in their hands, to be presented to their wives for the beautification of the impending Sabbath.

But on the Friday morning of June 7, 1968, as I stood at the sink brushing my teeth in preparation for work, a fellow volunteer came up to me and said, "We're not working today. It's a new holiday: Jerusalem Day."

"What's that?" I wondered.

"On this day last year, we conquered Jerusalem, so the government has declared it a national holiday. Our friends on the other side of the valley are sure to start some fireworks, but what they don't know is that the kibbutz will be empty. We're going out to the fields for a parachute jump."

"A what?" I asked.

"Many of the boys from this and the neighboring kibbutz are Tzanḥanim: army parachutists. They need to do a practice jump every so often, so today they're going to put on a show for us."

As the sun rose, seven trucks lined up near the office in the kibbutz parking lot. When I arrived, I stood back and watched as older members of the kibbutz, along with some younger women with children, loaded themselves into the trucks for the first trip up to the fields. After a lumbering journey of about a half hour each way, the trucks were to return to pick up the rest: younger members, volunteers, and some invited guests. Each truck had four rows of fold-up wooden benches in the covered rear bed—two inner rows facing outward and two outer rows facing inward—and could carry a maximum of forty-eight passengers, twelve to a row.

When it was my turn, I was among the last to board. "My good fortune," I muttered to myself as I took my seat at the end of an outer row.

From this vantage point, I could look out over the truck's rear gate to watch as the verdant Jordan Valley gradually disappeared below. The scene was one of breathtaking beauty.

As my truck made its way up to the plateau of Issachar, it arrived at a recently harvested wheat field, where the stubble had been disked and raked—too early for planting but smoothed out perfectly as a paratrooper landing field.

A man was standing in front of the crowd speaking into a microphone as I climbed down off the truck. Soon the sound of airplane engines could be heard in the distance. As the World War II–era planes approached, they made a pass over the field and circled around. On the second pass, parachutes began to open up. As each paratrooper floated to the ground, the announcer told the crowd which of their fellow kibbutzniks was coming to land on the field. As they neared the ground and their names were announced a second time, some of the men would make a scissor or frog-kick motion with their legs or pretend they were running on air. As each one landed, the crowd applauded.

Shimon had moved over toward me to watch the show. He glanced about, then leaned in close. "Last year, in the Sinai, a member of their regiment came down as a *ner*," he whispered quietly.

I recognized the Hebrew word meaning "candle," but I must have looked confused. Shimon demonstrated the concept by raising his arm over his head, cupping his hand into a nearly closed fist, and bringing it straight down in front of him.

"Like a *ner*," he said. "His parachute failed to open. The boys are still getting over it, so this practice, with all the attention, is also therapy for them."

A few weeks later, the bomb shelter trenches were completed, and it was time for the grape harvest. This normally pastoral occupation was dangerous work, however, in Kibbutz Haziv's vineyards along the Jordan River in 1968.

While the kibbutz had been built on a plateau a couple of hundred yards to the west of the river, Haziv's vineyards were planted in the fertile soil along the river in the valley below. In this particular area, the Jordan River was just a ten-foot-wide stream most of the year. Over the millennia, the river had carved out the fertile valley where kibbutz grapes now grew. The Jordanians sat on a plateau on their side, much closer to the river, above a hundred-foot cliff. Palestinians on the Jordanian side thus towered over the valley and had a much better strategic outlook.

Each morning, my coworkers—volunteers, kibbutzniks, and some soldiers—and I hopped onto a flatbed trailer pulled by a tractor. As part of a slow-moving caravan, we rode from the kibbutz to the vineyards in the valley below, proceeded first by a steamroller with long arms to explode mines planted by the enemy overnight, then by a half-track filled with soldiers and .50-caliber mounted machine guns. Once the dirt tracks were cleared of mines, and once the half-track had taken its position behind a sandbagged barrier facing the Jordanian plateau, the tractor would slowly pull us into the valley—under the watchful eye of the PLO, who were in turn carefully scrutinized by the IDF soldiers in the half-track.

Other IDF soldiers in stationary positions, we were told, were out there with us, hidden from view. This military standoff coupled with the summer heat made the eight-hour workday in the vineyards uncomfortably intense.

The kibbutz maintained good relations with the three Israeli-Arab villages in the region: Tamra, Na'ura, and Taibe. They were among the nearly one hundred Palestinian villages whose Arab residents, I was told, chose not to flee during the War of Independence. Following the war, the Arab villagers became Israeli citizens with all the attendant privileges and responsibilities but were understandably exempt from compulsory army service.

"We don't want them to have to fight against their cousins," Shimon said.

Some local Arab villagers worked in the kibbutz, received decent wages and benefits, and belonged to the national labor union. Kibbutzniks would be invited to special celebrations—weddings, for example—in these Arab villages, and on occasion, they would invite their Arab neighbors to similar celebrations on the kibbutz. There were even Israeli-Arab representatives in the Knesset, the parliament.

Shimon continued to explain, "The one hundred and sixty thousand Arabs who stayed after 1948 accepted our offer of citizenship, and Arabic became one of our three official languages. We've always had good relations with most of our Arab neighbors. They have prospered along with us and have a relatively high standard of living—but I don't know what they have in their hearts."

Such was life in a kibbutz along the Jordan River, south of the Sea of Galilee, in the first three years following the Six-Day War. In time, the frequent skirmishes along this front, as well as along the Suez Canal boundary with Egypt, acquired a name. It became known as Milḥemet Hahatasha—the War of Attrition.

But the fighting—at least along the Jordan Valley—came to an abrupt end in September 1970, when Palestinian terrorists hijacked three foreign airliners—Swissair, TWA, and BOAC—and forced them to fly to Amman, Jordan. When all the passengers had been released, the PLO blew up the planes in front of a whole host of television cameras.

With that, King Hussein of Jordan had had enough. Following these audacious acts, he declared that Jordan would no longer tolerate a fifth column operating within his kingdom. He unleashed his formidable army against the PLO and forced them to flee northward to Beirut.

The king—who had joined Egypt, Syria, and Iraq in the Six-Day War and lost East Jerusalem and the entire West Bank in the process—had more or less looked the other way when the cross-border skirmishes between the PLO and Israel first erupted in the war's aftermath. But at the same time, he had maintained secret contacts with Israel concerning peace and security along their common border. His grandfather, King Abdullah, had been assassinated in 1951 for making similar peaceful overtures toward Israel, but this did not impede ongoing clandestine contact between the two governments.

One day, in fact, I noticed a flurry of unusual activity among members of the kibbutz.

"What's going on?" I asked my friend Michael Azaria, who was close to me in age and had excellent command of English.

Michael put his index finger to his lips, whispering, "King Hussein's cousin, the Jordanian agricultural minister, is here to look at Monyak's egg operation."

Manis "Monyak" Adelman, an experienced egg farmer from Upstate New York, had come to Kibbutz Haziv with the intention of teaching its poultry farmers how to increase egg production. His mechanized operation could produce three times the number of eggs, though it occupied only about one-fifth the floor space of a typical set of henhouses and required only half the manpower. The hens were kept in a cage and given all their nutrition and medication via conveyor belt. A second conveyer belt carried their eggs away for packing.

It wasn't exactly the most humane operation—a far cry from the green notion of free range, which would later come into vogue. But it was a very effective and efficient enterprise. And somehow news of this American technology crossed the Jordan River frontier, even in the midst of a military conflict.

Within a quarter century, Israel would be at peace with her neighbor, the Hashemite Kingdom of Jordan.

I was fortunate to witness a small part of the evolution of that relationship.

CHAPTER VIII.

 KIBBUTZ HAZIV. 1970.

Behold: He winnows barley tonight on the threshing floor.

RUTH 3:2

W hen I returned to the kibbutz two years later with a bach-
elor's degree in history, I was elevated to the position of
cereal grain tractorist, an assignment for which not even a driver's
license was required. But the thought of being overeducated never
entered my mind. I was in love with the land and its people, its
geography, its history, its ideals, and its spirit.

I would rise every day at 3:30 a.m.; don my work clothes; front
up to the dining room at 3:50; sit down with my fellow workers
for a cup of Turkish coffee, appropriately called *café botz* ("mud
coffee"); pick up my paper-sacked breakfast; hop in a jeep; and
drive up the serpentine road overlooking the Jordan Valley to the
plateau of Issachar. There I would find my green-and-yellow John
Deere 830 awaiting my arrival, all gassed up and ready to go.

After four hours of work, I would stop the tractor, walk up
the nearest rise, and wrap myself in my tefillin and prayer shawl.
Turning southward toward Jerusalem—with the Jezreel Valley in
the foreground and the mountains of Samaria on the horizon—I

would then recite the brief morning prayer as recorded in Book of Deuteronomy, a Hebrew passage from Moses's charge to the Israelites as they made ready to cross the Jordan River to settle the Promised Land:

> *Shma Yisrael Adonai Eloheynu Adonai Eḥad*—Hear, O Israel, Adonai is our God, Adonai alone. Thou shalt love the Lord thy God with all thy heart, with all thy soul, and with all thy might. Take to heart these instructions with which I charge thee this day. Thou shalt teach them diligently to thy children, speaking of them when thou sittest in thy house, when thou walkest by the way, when thou risest up and when thou liest down. And thou shalt bind them for a sign upon thine hand. And they shall be as frontlets between thine eyes. And thou shalt inscribe on the doorposts of thy house and upon the gates of your cities. That you may remember them and perform all of my commandments and be holy unto Thy God.

When I finished praying, I would sit on the ground, prop myself up against one of the huge tractor tires, and wolf down my breakfast. I felt sorry for the kitchen staff, who had to awaken even earlier than I to prepare those paper sacks full of kibbutz delicacies: half of a baked chicken, which I would describe as a "half-baked chicken" when I wrote home; a bottle of Tempo orange soda; a bread roll; an orange or a grapefruit; and a chunk of marbled halvah.

Four hours later, when my shift was over, I would hop back in the jeep and return to the kibbutz for lunch and a nap. During harvest time, the tractor would operate twenty-four hours each day, in three eight-hour shifts, so I would, on occasion, be called to perform some small task in the afternoon as well.

Once in a while, I would ride up to the fields early in the morning with another kibbutznik who needed the jeep that day and be picked up by him at the end of my shift. One such day, my friend and farming mentor, Michael—who chose to befriend me, I think, at least initially out of a desire to practice his English—was waiting with the jeep a full half hour before my shift was due to end.

"I'm going to teach you how to make your rows straighter," Michael explained. "Now, look over there, in the distance. Do you see that cone-shaped mountain? That's Sartaba—you know, the place where they lit the bonfire to signal the new moon."

I did not know. But years later, I would find the reference in the Talmud. In ancient Israel, when the new moon was sighted just before sundown, a bonfire would be lit on Mount Scopus in Jerusalem. When that bonfire was seen at Sartaba, twenty-five miles to the north, men of that area would ascend the mountain and light their bonfire to signal communities farther to the north—and so on and so forth throughout the Fertile Crescent. That is how they reckoned the days in biblical times, by counting from the new moon.

"Just aim the center of your tractor, always, at Sartaba when you're heading south," Michael continued, "then follow the line on your return pass. That way, your rows will be straight. It has to do with parallax. By the way," he added, "the lands you are working are called Ramot Issachar, the hills of Issachar. They were part of

Joshua's allotment to the tribe of Issachar. The deed is recorded in the Book of Joshua, chapter nineteen, if you want to look it up."

Fascinating, I thought. Michael possessed no more than a high school education, but his schooling had given him an excellent grasp of the English language and familiarity with the Hebrew Bible and Talmud as well. In five minutes, Michael had spanned over a thousand years of Jewish history, from Joshua's division of the land to the Talmud's bonfires heralding the new moon.

I had always loved Jewish history, especially when it was touched on in high school or college. But now it began to dawn on me that this is where that history came alive.

Current events came alive too, when a low-flying Israeli jet on its way to Lebanon would fly just out of reach as I drove my tractor. When that happened, I would stop the tractor and stand on the seat. That way, I could catch a glimpse of the pilot in the cockpit as he maneuvered his A-4 Skyhawk along the contours of the terrain to avoid enemy radar. The next day, more often than not, I would read about the sortie in the newspaper. From the Bible to the Talmud, to the exploits of the vaunted Israeli Air Force, on the hills of Issachar, I watched history unfold before me.

One late afternoon, Michael asked me to take the jeep up to a newly harvested field to move the large rolling fuel storage container to another field for the next day's work. There I came upon an astonishing scene. Women from a nearby Arab village were sitting in the field around a pile of grain they had gleaned from that day's mechanized kibbutz harvest. Into the air above their heads, they tossed stalks of grain that had escaped the harvester.

I was amazed at what I saw: a passage from my own Bar Mitzvah Torah portion coming to life before my very eyes! The passage, from the Book of Leviticus, contained the law of *peah*, or corners:

"And when you reap the harvest of your land, you shall not wholly reap the corners of your field, neither shall you gather the gleanings of your harvest . . . you shall leave them for the poor and the stranger." It eventually became the basis for an entire corpus of Jewish law concerning charitable giving and social welfare.

The Arab women I happed upon that late afternoon were tossing up handfuls of grain to separate the heavier wheat (which would fall back to the ground) from the chaff (which would be carried off by the wind). It was a scene right out of the Hebrew Bible, as if nothing had changed in twenty-five hundred years.

I sat quietly in my jeep and watched as the women gathered the winnowed wheat in cloth sheets they had laid on the ground. They bundled them up and carried them over their shoulders as they walked off in the direction of their village. Only then did I perform the task to which I had been assigned.

The next day when I returned from my work a little early, I was sent right back to pick up a kibbutz member harvesting another area. I hadn't seen very much of this tall, fair-haired man around the village, but this was harvest time, so it was all hands on deck. He was about a decade older than I and clearly an exceptional farmer. He liked to work overtime, I was told.

But as I approached his field, I was appalled by what I saw. This kibbutznik, having finished the field, was now walking over the entire area with a scythe, cutting down and gathering up every bit of grain on that entire plot of land, gleaning every last shaft of wheat. Though we hadn't been introduced and I had never before spoken to him, when he entered the jeep, I could not contain myself.

"Don't you know about the law of *peah*?" I chided the farmer, whom I only knew by his nickname, Banjo. "You are supposed to leave the corners for the poor."

I was a bit surprised when he answered me with what sounded like a flat cockney accent.

"Listen here, young man," he said. "This wheat belongs to us, every bit of it."

"No, I don't think it does," I said boldly.

"And who do you think it belongs to? These Arabs?"

"I think it belongs to God." I was surprised to find the words coming so effortlessly from my lips. I had never spoken of God in that way. "And you need to learn to share it. Who provided the rain, the sunshine, the soil, after all? Did you?"

We sat in strained silence for the duration of the journey back to the kibbutz. As I drove, I wondered how the Arab women would react upon approaching the field that afternoon, only to find it picked clean by a greedy kibbutz farmer.

Over time, I would become a competent tractorist. I could prepare a field for planting as quickly as any experienced kibbutz farmer. I learned to care for my tractor and could plow, disk, and rake quite adeptly. My fieldwork secured my place in the kibbutz workforce at least for the warm summer months and well into the fall planting season.

But as it turned out, the newly acquired cultivation skills did not automatically endear me to all my fellow farmers.

CHAPTER IX.

 KIBBUTZ HAZIV. 1971–73.

Both sides of any disagreement are usually right in their own way.

RUTH CALDERON, KNESSET MEMBER

B enjamin Braham was an Australian-born Israeli. He was tall and muscular, ruggedly handsome—a man with a military bearing who though on the verge of middle age looked much younger. Banjo, as he was known among the members of Kibbutz Haziv, was well liked both by the men and the women of the community.

Having lived on the kibbutz for more than twenty years, he could perform almost all the essential tasks. He would fill in wherever needed but spent most of his time as a tractorist in the *falḥa*—cereal grain fields—and a dairyman in the *refet*—the dairy.

But the curious thing about Banjo Braham, at least according to my then-unschooled scrutiny, was his disappearance from the kibbutz for days and sometimes weeks at a time. His family—wife, Yael, and two daughters—sat at their regular table in the dining room every evening, but Banjo would often be noticeably absent.

When I inquired, Michael's face cracked into a mysterious smile, and he said only, "He helps out the government."

"Why do they call him Banjo?" I wanted to know.

"I wasn't here at the time, of course," Michael explained, "but they tell me that when he arrived just after the end of the Second World War, he had a big round belly, probably from malnourishment, and a long skinny neck. His name was Benjamin, and he was shaped like a banjo, so that's what they called him. As you can see, he's worked hard to change his shape, and he parades around now to show us how successful he's been at it. But try as he might to outlive the nickname, it seems he's saddled with it forever."

Banjo Braham was a bit of a legend in the territory. The word around the village was that he had been part of Ariel Sharon's fabled Unit 101, a special forces group that made occasional forays into either the Jordanian-occupied West Bank or the Egyptian-occupied Gaza Strip.

Another rumor had it that Banjo was one of only a handful of Israelis who brazenly slipped across the border to trek deep into Jordan and touch the "Red Rock," known more widely as Petra, the storied Jordanian archaeological site that in a more peaceful time would become a setting for the film *Indiana Jones and the Last Crusade*.

Banjo's few good friends knew the truth about the rumors, but they would "neither confirm nor deny." As my friend Michael's wry smile seemed to imply, though, Banjo's current offsite activities had nothing to do with Unit 101 or Petra, but rather with Israel's vaunted Institute for Intelligence and Special Operations: the Mossad.

While most kibbutz members might admire Benjamin Braham for his bravery, they did not necessarily agree with his politics nor with his impetuous action against their nearest neighbor, the Palestinian village of Kafr Laisa, when he was only a boy.

Perched on a plateau above Haziv, a little to the south, Kafr Laisa was one of the many Arab villages abandoned in 1948. On occasion, I would walk among its ruins and marvel at the view of the Jordan Valley below.

Before the war, Kafr Laisa had been comprised of thirty-some small stone houses with red tile roofs, a post office, a small grocery store, a machine shop, a mosque, a school, and a community hall. The largest house belonged to the sheikh of the village, a distant relative of Haj Amin al-Husseini, the grand mufti of Jerusalem, an ally of Adolf Hitler who opposed Jewish immigration to British Mandatory Palestine.

Even though all the land belonging to pre-state Israel had been purchased from its legal owners, the members of Kafr Laisa did not want Jewish neighbors, to put it mildly. During the anti-Jewish-immigration riots of 1936, shots were fired from Laisa down on Haziv, causing a serious injury and a minor injury before fire was returned and calm restored. After that, relations between the two communities, never warm to begin with, remained uncomfortably strained.

Why did the people of Kafr Laisa abandon their village in 1948? I asked that very question to Shimon Reinfeld one day.

"Once the British announced their decision to leave the region," he explained, "the Palestinian military leadership ordered out the old people, the women, and the children of Kafr Laisa. They planned an attack on our kibbutz and didn't want the people of Laisa to get in their way—they didn't want to be responsible for any 'collateral damage.' The British gladly complied—some would say colluded—with the Palestinian military, hoping the new Arab State of Palestine would become a strong British ally when the war was over.

"So in March 1948, six British lorries drove up the hill and evacuated the old people, the women, and the children of the village. I saw it with my own eyes. The men were left to guard the buildings and the fields. But just before the real fighting started, they abandoned the village too. We asked them to stay. Uriel Dagan and Gur Aryeh even went up there to ask the sheikh not to leave, but they left anyway.

"I think most Palestinians were led to believe the evacuation would be temporary—that they would return to their homes in the wake of the victorious Arab Legion. It didn't turn out that way, of course," he added with a confident smile.

"But what about Tamra and Na'ura and the—what did you tell me—one hundred other Arab villages? Why are all those Arabs still here? Why didn't they flee?"

I was puzzled. The story I had been led to believe was that the Jews won and all the Arabs fled.

"It's simple," Shimon replied. "The other villages weren't in the way. The Arab Legion knew, more or less, where they would attack. We had our battle plans too. Most Arab civilians who fled were encouraged to leave potential battle zones. Sometimes we encouraged them in ways their leaders did not. Other civilians, fearing nothing from us, stayed in place. It happened to us as well. My cousins, for example, abandoned their homes in East Jerusalem when the legion attacked. It happens that way pretty much, I suppose, in every war."

After a month of fighting, the first truce was declared in June 1948. Twelve-year-old Banjo Braham took the kibbutz's D6 bulldozer up to Kafr Laisa and knocked down every building.

"I wanted to make sure those bloody Arabs wouldn't come back," he later told me with a certain degree of pride.

Banjo didn't like Americans very much either. He considered them spoiled, loud, and lazy. He made it clear to me that his disdain for Americans had a long history, beginning when American GIs arrived en masse in his hometown of Brisbane, Australia, after the attack on Pearl Harbor.

Over one million American service personnel passed through Australia during the Second World War, among them General Douglas MacArthur following his setback in the Philippines. In the four years of American involvement in the Pacific, northern Australia became the premier locale for American servicemen on furlough—a preferred spot for rest, convalescence, and relaxation. They brought their own American culture with them: soda fountains and nightclubs and cafés that served them American-style meals. They were better paid; lived in better housing; and through the system of PX, or post exchange, stores had access to much better consumer goods than their Australian counterparts.

The Aussies, on the other hand, had been left to fend for themselves by the British military of which they were a part. Britain's empire was simply too vast to defend, so the king depended on his American Allies to protect, as well as they could, his Antipodean and Asian colonies from Japanese aggression.

At first, the Americans were welcomed as saviors. Australian women tended to see the well-paid, casual, easygoing Americans as romantic and desirable. But over time, some of the glamour wore off. From the unenamored Aussie point of view, here were these spoiled, carefree Americans gallivanting around the city streets while Aussie soldiers, along with their New Zealand brothers, were suffering and dying for Mother England.

A considerable number of Australians grew to resent the Americans, even though they well knew their country could not adequately defend itself in the face of a possible Japanese invasion. The Japanese attack on their northern city of Darwin in February 1942 convinced them of that. So although the American presence was considered a strategic necessity, the locals grew fond of saying, "Americans are overpaid, oversexed, and, unfortunately, over here!"

Anti-American sentiment bubbled over in November 1942 in the Battle of Brisbane, a large-scale riot between Australian and American servicemen—which six-year-old Benjamin Braham witnessed from his home at the edge of Brisbane's central business district. One Australian soldier was dead and a number of Americans and Australians were injured before peace was restored.

Rumor had it that Banjo's mother became involved with an American GI while Banjo's father was fighting overseas. Evidently, the American abandoned both mother and child when the war ended, but Benjamin had hated the American from the very beginning, especially after learning his father had died in the Japanese prison camp at Changi, Singapore.

His mother never recovered from the double tragedy of losing both men. When she died just after the war's end, the orphaned Banjo was brought to Israel under the Youth Aliyah program, along with dozens of young European Holocaust survivors.

Grief and resentment came to inform Banjo's entire attitude toward Americans, and I suffered for it. When Banjo organized a kibbutz excursion down to the Israeli side of the Suez Canal, for example, I received a rude awakening that let me know just where I stood with him.

I was by then a candidate for membership in the kibbutz and among the first to sign up for the trip. But after a few days, word came down to me along the kibbutz grapevine: the tour of the Suez Canal would be for Israeli citizens only. "Security" was the purported rationale, but I sensed something more personal in the edict. Even though I had already visited sensitive IDF outposts on the Golan Heights border with Syria, had faced gunfire and mortar fire from the Jordanian side of the river, and would soon be trained at the Sarafand army base, I was suddenly disqualified from this trip. I felt certain Banjo was behind the decision, and my own animosity toward the Australian grew more intense.

"Are you ready for your army training?" Michael asked me after the fall harvest during my second year of residency. "We need more men to do guard duty. There's a training course for temporary kibbutz residents starting next week."

I tried to be nonchalant, but inside I was thrilled. I already knew I would be required to complete some basic training once I declared my intention to remain on the kibbutz indefinitely. I also knew that service in Israel's army was the dividing line between those who were "in" in Israeli society and those who would forever remain "outside," even if they were naturalized citizens. After this smattering of training, I would still not fully qualify as an insider, but it would help.

A week later, I made my way by bus to the former British army base at Sarafand and checked into the doctor's office for my physical. Over the course of the next two weeks, I learned how to shoot the long-ranged, single-shot, bolt-action "Czechy," an old-fashioned rifle with an effective range of up to five hundred meters. The Czechys had been provided to the fledgling Haganah military force through a post–World War II arms deal. I also learned how to break into a building where terrorists would be hiding, how to set up a field of fire, how to estimate distances, how to advance and cover.

Most importantly, I learned how to use the Uzi submachine gun, an Israeli-made nine-millimeter weapon with an effective range of one hundred meters and a thirty-two-round clip for village guard duty. By the end of the ten-day course, I could break down and reassemble the Uzi faster than anyone else in the class.

My brief stint at the Sarafand base also included a measure of informal ideological instruction. Some more cynical class members called it "indoctrination," but I was among those already sold on the justice of Israel's cause well before signing up for the training.

My instructor was a young man named Gaulani, who had lived in Vienna for a time with his diplomat father. Gaulani told the class how he had witnessed the first tentative groups of Soviet Jewish émigrés arriving in Vienna in the late '60s. They had lived their lives under Communist oppression, made even more acute when they began to express their desire to leave the Soviet "paradise."

Gaulani's voice rose in volume and pitch when he told the story; at times he sounded positively evangelic. "*Zeh hayah Y'tziat Mitzraim,*" he related to us with great enthusiasm, his eyes bulging. "It was just like the Exodus from Egypt. When they came off the trains in Vienna, they knelt down and kissed the ground!"

His passion was contagious. We trainees came to identify with our leader, to accept his conviction that this mission—bringing Jews to their homeland—was the ultimate goal of our training and that this was, in fact, the very reason Israel had come into existence. I easily became one of Gaulani's most committed recruits.

Looking back on those days, I came to realize that this brief spell at the Sarafand army base was the high point of my romance with Israel. Soon thereafter, the discordant reality of post-'67 Israel would cause me to tumble out of love and come to grips with my need to plot an alternate life course.

It all came to a head when Banjo, on leave from his "other" job, was invited to join a small group of young men, myself among them, for our daily late-afternoon tea. As always, the discussion came around to current events—the relative quiet along the Suez border, air force sorties, the upcoming kibbutz general meeting, and relations with the neighboring Kingdom of Jordan—when Banjo suddenly blurted out, "The only good Arab is a dead Arab."

By that time, I had already come far from the dream world of the '60s, but the gap between a naïve vision of world peace, love, and brotherhood and Banjo Braham's racist attitude became too much to bridge. Staring directly at Banjo across the circle, I broke into a mild rage.

"When you belittle your enemy, you belittle yourself! What are *you* that you can only defeat worthless human beings?" I countered to the amazement of the stunned gathering of men.

My logic, followed by an uncomfortable silence, seemed to have hit home. But it did not endear me to Banjo, to say the least—nor apparently to some of the other men of the kibbutz.

"You should see what they say about us!" Yossi chimed in. "They teach their kids math by counting dead Jews."

"We're better than that," I argued.

"So you're saying our culture is superior to theirs? Tell me—is there a big difference in the English language between *belittling* and *denigrating*?"

Yossi had a point.

"You Americans," Banjo soon shot back, "with your lofty ideals. Why don't you learn to live in the real world? You want us to give back the territories in return for peace. Well, let me ask you something: When the UN Partition Plan gave the Arabs half of Israel, why didn't they make peace then? There was no refugee problem in the beginning of 1948. Why did they attack us, instead, from all sides and try to drive us into the sea? Now they say if we just withdraw to the 1948 borders, there will be peace.

"So I ask you, if the 1948 lines weren't acceptable borders back then, before they launched the Six-Day War, why would they suddenly become acceptable in a peace agreement now? There was no 'occupation' before 1967, but there *was* constant terror, and a major war broke out.

"So don't be naïve, my American friend. They're scum. If the Arabs lay down their arms, okay—there will be no more war. But if *we* lay down *our* arms, there will be no more Israel! Of that you can be certain."

Their arguments were compelling, I had to admit to myself. And so, after entering the fray, I chose to clam up.

Over the years, I would come to understand that folks on the left, with whom I wholeheartedly identified back then, can at times be just as arrogant, narrow-minded, self-righteous, and intolerant as folks on the right. The BBC, for example, has as narrow an agenda as does Fox News.

In time, nonetheless, I would come to believe that my critique of Banjo and his ilk was somewhat prophetic, even if I do say so myself. You should never underestimate your enemy. The problem with Israel was a tendency to underestimate everyone—not only their enemies but even their allies and friends. A little more respect for the other side would have been a healthy quality to acquire.

In time, their carelessness would lead them into the Yom Kippur War and other serious international blunders, to which I would be an unwitting eyewitness.

CHAPTER X.

 JORDAN VALLEY. MARCH 1972.

Judah is a lion cub.

Genesis 49:9

Judah Gur Aryeh was already a kibbutz legend by the time I was introduced to him—so much so that the kibbutz featured him on their publicity postcards, standing under a tree in the grapefruit orchard with his wiry physique and distinctive Einstein-like wild white coif.

He was seventy-four years old when I first met him, and we immediately took a liking to each other. I idolized the old man from the moment I learned he was one of those pioneer dreamers who walked all the way from Russia to Israel in the early 1920s. I believed he, in turn, saw a bit of himself—and validation for his pioneering efforts—in this young American who had come to settle in the Promised Land.

When winter turned to spring and the fields were still too wet to work, the great spring trek dates were announced. These annual marches were grand public events whose entry fees would be used to support local charities, as in many other countries.

First, there was to be the challenging Gilboa March, a thirty-kilometer walk from the Bet Shean Valley up the side of Mount

Gilboa and back down again to Ma'ayan Ḥarod, the Ḥarod Spring, where the famous biblical general Gideon chose his soldiers for battle. The Gilboa March would be followed by the Mount Tabor Marathon a few weeks later, and that would be followed by the great three-day March to Jerusalem as a prelude to Passover.

To prepare for the Gilboa trek, Gur Aryeh suggested that he and I walk together from Kibbutz Haziv down Highway 90 to Bet Shean and back, a relatively flat distance of twenty-nine kilometers, or eighteen miles.

"Sure," I said, quite delighted by the invitation. "But isn't it dangerous?" I remembered with some apprehension my first bus ride along that road during the War of Attrition.

"Don't be afraid, my American friend. We can't be afraid in our own land," came Gur Aryeh's response. "And besides, it's much quieter now since the king chased away the PLO."

So side by side we marched south along the treelined highway: the seventy-four-year-old pioneer and the twenty-four-year-old college graduate from Minnesota. I was proud to be seen walking with the legendary pioneer, fascinating character that he was.

Down the Jordan Valley we walked, stopping at Bet Shean, the halfway point, for a picnic lunch by the side of the road before heading back up the valley.

At Bet Shean, Gur Aryeh pointed to the road that led westward toward the town of Afula.

"This is what I helped build when I first arrived in Ha-aretz," he declared, using the affectionate name for Israel, meaning "the Land." "They put us to work building roads and draining malarial swamps, right here in this valley. There was a lot of suffering during those years, but we were imbued with the pioneering spirit. Now see how fine this road looks, how fertile this valley appears."

"Didn't the harsh reality of Ha-aretz dampen your enthusiasm?" I asked, reflecting upon my own predicament.

"Only a little. We were under no illusions. Life in Russia was no picnic either, so it was easy for us to leave. We did not have any of the luxuries you have in America. And we were well prepared for the difficulties here—though I must admit, the malaria was an unexpected hardship. This was all swampland back then. We knew we were here for the long haul, and that's what made it easier, plus the fact that there were many of us. It's much easier to endure when you are all in the same boat."

With a gleam in his eye, he now turned toward me as we consumed our sack lunches on a bench under the Bet Shean city limit sign. "In addition, the girls among us were young and pretty. It was like the dawn of a whole new era. We took a lot of personal liberties back then, if you know what I mean."

Gur Aryeh then related a story about British journalist Edward Grant, one of the early wire photographers of London's *Daily Mirror*. He had come to Palestine between the two world wars to photograph a group of young Jewish pioneers who had settled near Jerusalem, building what was to eventually become Kibbutz Ramat Rachel just south of the city.

Each day, Grant reported, the kibbutzniks would awaken at daybreak, attach two large buckets to the ends of wooden yokes balanced on their shoulders, grab a shovel, and walk down to the valley below. Upon reaching the valley floor, they would load topsoil into their buckets, trudge back up to the top of the hill fully laden, then pour the fertile soil out along the terraced hillsides. Every day, throughout the daylight hours, for weeks on end, they would carry on in this fashion.

After observing and photographing this procedure for some time, Grant approached the kibbutz secretary and inquired, "What precisely are you trying to accomplish here?"

"Mr. Grant," the kibbutz secretary explained, "for centuries these Judean hills have been devoid of people. Through years of neglect, this topsoil washed down from these once-fertile hills and was deposited into the valley floor below. Now that we have returned to our homeland, we are bringing the soil back to where it belongs so these terraces can become productive once again."

"But," replied Grant incredulously, "it will take a hundred years to accomplish that." It was only a slight overstatement.

"Perhaps," the unfazed kibbutznik said. "But Mr. Grant, we've waited a long, long time to return to our homeland. What's another hundred years to the Jewish people?"

When Gur Aryeh and I finally arrived back in the vicinity of the kibbutz, we looked up toward the ruins of Kafr Laisa. It was a half-mile climb at an oblique angle. Given the eighteen miles we had already walked, it appeared quite daunting.

To my amazement, Gur Aryeh stopped in his tracks and removed two lead weights from his backpack. The old man then inserted the weights into small pockets he had sewn outside his ankle-high sneakers, adding two pounds to each foot. He snapped the pockets closed.

"I want this to be real exercise," he explained as he began to run straight uphill. "Keep up with me if you can," he yelled back as I soon fell far behind.

When I finally made it up the hill and back down to the kibbutz dining hall, a well-rested Gur Aryeh was waiting for me.

"Maybe we should do this once more before the big events begin," he suggested.

That day—for me, at least—the legend of Judah Gur Aryeh and an entire generation of young pioneers walking all the way from Russia to Palestine emerged from the realm of myth into the realm of actuality.

CHAPTER XI.

 KIBBUTZ HAZIV. JUNE 1972.

There is no love without chastisement.

TALMUD

The Six-Day War of 1967 brought six years of glory to Israel. For a brief moment in history, Israelis were larger than life, having won the admiration of the entire world. But behind the veil, I could already perceive the chimerical quality of that brief halcyon period. Even before the Yom Kippur War brought Israel down from her six-year euphoria, I had begun to grow disenchanted.

I had come there with my youthful idealism to escape the rampant materialism of capitalist America, but what I discovered in Israel was more of the same—but on steroids. I had come there imbued with a yearning for peace, firmly believing that if the Israel-Palestine problem could be resolved, any world conflict could be resolved. But I found that the long occupation—however justified—that followed the great victory was gradually eroding every ounce of goodwill between the two sides.

During my brief sojourn, I also witnessed the "beginning of the end of the kibbutz idea," as Michael described it when, in June 1972, the kibbutz voted by a slim majority to let one member stand out from all the rest.

The kibbutz was based on the pure communist notion, "From each according to his ability, to each according to his need." Each kibbutznik was provided with everything he or she needed from cradle to grave. The kibbutz owned everything except for the few small items an individual received as gifts or purchased out of a modest weekly "spending budget." A radio, for example, or a small television would be permitted. But a bathtub—no, not unless all bathrooms were remodeled to accommodate such a luxury, and that would be beyond the treasury's means.

To be sure, there were kibbutzniks who worked outside the village, but they contributed their entire salaries to the general fund. Tzvi Yamini was a case in point.

"Why is Tzvi Yamini washing pots and pans in the dish room?" I asked Michael after lunch one day. "Isn't he a sitting member of the Knesset?"

"Yes, he is," said Michael, "and he's a war hero as well. In fact, he's fought in all our wars. But that's what we do here on the kibbutz. Even the highest government minister—or the chief executive of the Jordan Valley Dairy Cooperative, to give you an example of another member—contributes his entire salary to the kibbutz. And when they have time off, they come back to the dish room and are assigned the most menial and difficult job: pots and pans. It's backbreaking, monotonous work, so having these 'bigwigs,' as you would call them, perform such tasks when they are off duty helps to equalize everything here on the kibbutz. No one, whatever his skills or level of fame, is more important than anyone else. We're all equal in the eyes of the kibbutz," he concluded with a sardonic smile.

So the capitalistic notion of having access to a private pension, instead of turning such investments over to the kibbutz treasury, ran counter to the entire philosophy of the kibbutz movement.

For weeks it was roundly discussed and hotly debated among kibbutz members, but in the end, Yosef Ron was allowed, by a slim majority vote, to keep the private pension money he had accrued as a bus driver for the Israel Transit Company. It was allowed first on Kibbutz Haziv, then on a number of other kibbutzim once the ground had been broken. Soon most kibbutzim would be transformed from collective communes to small rural villages in which the residents owned their own homes, their own appliances, and their own cars.

It was once said that the only place communism really worked was on a kibbutz in Israel. But after that decision on Kibbutz Haziv in 1972, the kibbutz of the twentieth century—a remarkable institution that gave Israel much of its early character—became a thing of the past.

"You'll see," kibbutz scholar Uriel Dagan told me a few days after the decisive vote. "Within a few years, the children's houses, where the entire community actively participates in the rearing of each child, will be a thing of the past. Gone too will be the committees working out which member's turn it will be to use the kibbutz car, or who will next be sent on a vacation abroad. Even the communal dining room, the social center of our entire kibbutz, will probably be gone. Gone along with all that will be our dedication to mutual aid and social justice, the sense of shared purpose, the renunciation of private property—the actual communal living that has fostered, better than any other system known to humankind, a real sense of equality."

It was not that socialism—the common economic system for the first thirty years of the tiny country's existence, of which the kibbutz was the most extreme form—was without flaw. Far from it. For instance, "the customer is always right" is a purely capitalist notion—and a good one at that, in my humble opinion. But in a socialist country such as Israel, the worker—backed by the union and ultimately the government—was always right. Not the customer.

This notion was brought home to me one day while standing in line at the Bet Shean National Bank. I had taken time off work to travel the fifteen kilometers to Bet Shean to deposit some of the spending-budget allowance I had saved. It was late in the workday, and the lone teller was particularly slow. Three people were still ahead of me at closing time when, at the precise moment the clock struck 4:00, the teller abruptly pulled down the wood-shutter panel, slammed his cage shut, and shouted out, "My eight hours are up. The bank is now closed. You will all have to come back tomorrow!"

I had been a wide-eyed fantasist weaned on the Labor Zionist myth, a product of the irrepressibly optimistic 1960s, wholly unprepared for the dystopian reality of Israel. The longer I stayed, the more distant from my dream the reality grew. After half a decade, I could no longer brook the rampant materialism of the middle class nor the economic stagnation of socialism, the murderous public behavior on the roads, or the stranglehold by which the religious minority held power over the secular majority. It was all too confusing, because at the same time, I had a hard time letting go of a certain degree of love and admiration for what Israel had accomplished in a very short time in its most inhospitable tiny corner of the world.

I guess I was not yet mature enough to have acquired a healthy degree of skepticism to balance my idealism, to appreciate that reality never quite measures up to the ideal. But that fact of life was beginning to make its appearance in my conscious mind.

Then came the Yom Kippur War.

CHAPTER XII.

 KIBBUTZ HAZIV. OCTOBER 1973.

The Land of Israel will be acquired through suffering.

Talmud

Four young men from Kibbutz Haziv—including my best friend and mentor, infantry reservist Michael Azaria—were posted on the Golan Heights at Tel Farid, a fortress carved into a hillock less than seventy-five yards from the border with Syria. It was early October 1973, on the eve of the Yom Kippur War. The comings and goings of vehicles at Tel Farid were clearly visible from the Syrian side across the narrow strip of no-man's-land. The reverse was also true.

For three days before Yom Kippur, the men of Haziv regularly reported on unusual Syrian maneuvers to their commander, Benjamin Braham, who had been called to headquarters at Nafah junction, some five kilometers behind the front lines. On the morning of Yom Kippur, they radioed to Banjo that the Syrians had moved mine-clearing tanks and bridge-layers right up to the border.

Banjo radioed back, "Do not worry. These are just maneuvers. In the highly unlikely event that they try to attack, you'll have plenty of backup. Don't worry."

But at 2:05 p.m. that afternoon, Michael's voice was loud and urgent on the radio. "They've crossed into no-man's-land! There are twenty or thirty tanks headed straight toward us. We can't hold them off with what we have. Banjo, unless you move your tanks up, we're abandoning our post!"

"*Stay where you are!*" Banjo snapped back in his most commanding voice. "I'm on my way to assess the situation. Do not retreat. I repeat: *do not move!*"

A few minutes later, Michael's panicked voice crackled over the radio. "They're crossing over the antitank ditches! They're working the minefields. We're firing at them now with everything we've got. Where are you? Where are the tanks? Where are the reserves?" Michael was pleading now.

"*Stay where you are!*" Banjo thundered. "I've got other things to worry about. Hold your position *at all costs*! Keep this line open. I'm on Tapline Road. "

But when Colonel Benjamin Braham's jeep climbed a short hill on Tapline Road less than a mile from Tel Farid, he saw a swarm of Syrian T-54 tanks surrounding the Tel in the valley below. He abruptly turned tail and raced back to Nafaḥ headquarters.

As he flew along the uneven road, Banjo heard voices from Tel Farid shouting over the radio. He could hear gunfire in the background. The voices, now clearer, were shouting in Arabic. A few more single shots were heard and then static. The radio went dead.

When Banjo, with his big guns, finally counterattacked three days later, he reached Tel Farid and found the bloated bodies of Michael, Zevy, Yoav, and Neḥemia among others lying near the rear entrance of the fortress. The smell of black powder and rotting flesh befouled the fresh mountain air. Burned-out Syrian tanks—their blackened turrets turned in all directions, their gun barrels pointing at grotesque angles—smoldered all around the Tel. The charred bodies of Syrian soldiers lay in and around their tanks. A pulverized IDF half-track lay in pieces nearby. It was a gruesome sight.

I did my best to offer words of comfort to Michael's parents. When they asked, "Why do the good die young?" I could only offer, "God needs a strong cadre of angels to help him take care of heaven." I had heard my father say something like that, but the words didn't seem to have any effect on Michael's parents. They were avowed atheists, after all.

In the end, all I could do was sit with them. It seemed to help a bit.

By the end of the first few days of the Yom Kippur War, it became clear that Israel would soon run out of equipment and supplies. That led to what many consider Richard Nixon's finest hour.

At his command, a huge emergency airlift dubbed "Operation Nickel Grass" was ordered. The United States Air Force airlifted twenty-two thousand tons of aircraft, tanks, ammunition, and supplies to Israel—without which the Jewish state would certainly have lost the war. No one has ever confirmed this for me, but I believe the designation "Nickel Grass" was chosen to signify "Nixon-Golda," the last name of the American president and the first name of the Israeli prime minister.

The 349th Military Airlift Wing, based at Travis Air Force Base in Northern California—which by sheer coincidence I would one day join as a volunteer base chaplain—played a major role in the US military airlift that helped turn the war around. The resupply enabled Israel to push the Syrians off the Golan Heights, encircle Egypt's Third Army, and eventually threaten both Damascus and Cairo.

During the war, I worked eight-hour shifts guarding the kibbutz through each long, uncertain night. I then caught as much sleep as I could before I hopped on my tractor to work alongside some elderly members and high school boys to first bring in the fall harvest, then plant the winter crop.

When the war was finally over, I was assigned to the dish room to face a gloomy winter. Although peace talks were taking place on Egyptian soil and Israel was to sign disengagement agreements with both Egypt and Syria in 1974, these developments did nothing at all to lift my spirits nor the spirits of the nation.

An Israeli commission was established immediately after the Yom Kippur War with a remittal to investigate the handling of intelligence information and frontline reports from the days before the war, as well as the army's state of readiness and its operations in the first days of combat. The commission's report, published in April 1974, blamed faulty intelligence and arrogance for the initial failures. It called for the dismissal of a number of senior officers of the IDF and caused such controversy that Prime Minister Golda Meir was forced to resign.

But for the Yom Kippur debacle on Tel Farid, for the death of Michael Azaria and the others, I soon discovered there would be no punishment and no accountability for the one person who was clearly to blame. Regarding the behavior of Colonel Benjamin Braham, the report would only briefly note, "He failed to order a tactical retreat at the proper time but otherwise fulfilled his duties adequately."

Unlike after the Six-Day War, Israel was in no mood to celebrate. In contrast, the Yom Kippur War inaugurated a period of gloom throughout the Holy Land. Four times as many IDF soldiers had died, and many more were wounded. The Six-Day War had placed Israel in a kind of optimistic daydream; the Yom Kippur War constituted a rude awakening from that dream. Although Israel snatched a huge victory from the jaws of defeat, the sobering effects of the Yom Kippur War have shaped its political landscape ever since.

In the aftermath of the war, a dark pall seemed to envelop the entire country, and I would soon be shrouded by it.

CHAPTER XIII.

 KIBBUTZ HAZIV. MAY 1974.

Who looks outside, dreams; who looks inside, awakes.

CARL JUNG

In May 1974, Shimon Reinfeld, my kibbutz "father," came to me with some surprising news.

"I have submitted your name for kibbutz membership," Shimon told me. "I hope that's what you wanted. If you have no objection, you will be voted on in the next general meeting."

"Well, yes! That's great," I replied to the unexpected news.

Up to this time, my official status had been that of a *m'umad*, a candidate for membership. I had been required to undergo a kind of trial period, undefined in length, to see how well I fit in with the others, what kind of worker I was, whether there were any serious personal problems. Now I had a chance to become a full-fledged member.

Perhaps this was what I was waiting for, a "sign from above" pointing to the direction my life should take. Upon further reflection, I also realized that the kibbutz had recently lost four young men and, though still mourning the severe loss, was now ready to consider accepting new members.

I stayed up late the night of the general meeting, which, for good reasons, I was not allowed to attend. No one came to tell me how the vote went, though, and I didn't want to put anyone in an uncomfortable position by asking the question point blank.

But when I went out to the dining room at 3:50 in the morning, Shimon, to my great surprise, was waiting for me. An uncomfortable silence followed our morning greetings.

Finally, I spoke up. "*Nu*, Shimon, how did it go last night?"

"Not so well, I'm afraid," was Shimon's hesitant response. "I'm afraid one or two people were able to sway the entire group against you."

I was shocked. For years, I had been building up to this moment, and it felt as if I had been punched in the stomach.

"Was it about anything specific that I've done?" I asked weakly. The news had taken the wind out of my sails.

"No, Jonathan. I'm afraid it was more about something you said on more than one occasion that some members felt was an indication of your general attitude," came Shimon's vague response. "Here we have to rely on each other, and at times, we have to put our lives in the hands of our friends. One or two of the men felt they would not be able to count on you when the chips were down."

Banjo Braham! I thought to myself. *He's had it out for me since the day I arrived.* I bit my tongue and said nothing but knew in my heart that my kibbutz days were numbered.

As the sun came up that morning, I realized my dream was vanishing in the light of the day. I had been rejected for kibbutz membership and would soon have to leave. I had nothing to offer the young state, had no real job prospects outside the kibbutz, and was so depressed I didn't even have the strength to look for employment. My good friend and mentor had died for no good reason. The shock of the Yom Kippur War moved Israel to the right as the Labor Party, the peace party, lost more and more seats in the Knesset. I was clearly at a crossroads.

Uriel Dagan, the scholar of Kibbutz Haziv, sensed my predicament. In a valiant effort to cheer me up, he told me a story:

An old man, well into his nineties, had been fighting off death for years. Finally exhausted, he pleads with God in a dream: "God, I'm ready to let go of this world. I will give up the struggle tomorrow if you will just show me what awaits me on the other side."

God consents and takes him to a land where people are joyfully skiing in perfect, newly fallen white powder in the morning; swimming in warm, clear-blue waters in the afternoon; sitting at the feet of great scholars in the evening; and dancing all night long. Everyone is content; no one is unhappy. And everyone is in the pink of health.

When he awakens, the man speaks to God in his morning prayer: "Okay, God, you can take me now." And right then and there in the synagogue chapel, he dies.

The next day he is transported to a place where it's burning hot during the day and freezing cold at night; where people throw their garbage in the streets; where factories pollute the air; where everyone complains about the slightest inconvenience; where they make rude comments to one another; where they elbow their way to the head of the line, argue all the time, and are satisfied with nothing.

The disillusioned man goes to God and says, "God, why have you brought me to *this* place? When I was still alive and asked you to show me the other side, you brought me to a veritable Garden of Eden; this place is pure hell."

"It's really quite simple," God answers. "Last time you came as a tourist."

The story just about summed it up for me. In the spring of 1974, in the wake of the Yom Kippur debacle, my dream came to an abrupt end. Israel was still a remarkable place, and what its citizens, despite all their shortcomings, accomplished in the first few decades of the country's existence was quite remarkable. But I came to realize that the day-to-day reality of life in the State of Israel was a far cry from the Israel I had been weaned on. Like the vast majority of the world's Jews, I might continue to love Israel from afar, but it was no longer a place I wanted to live in.

So, in the late summer of 1974, I, Jonathan Jacob Kadison, having failed as a kibbutz member, decided to fall back on my reserves and go into the family business. Like my father before me, I left the Holy Land to become a rabbi in America.

PART II
NORTH BAY

CHAPTER XIV.

 NORTH BAY, CALIFORNIA.

DECEMBER 1977.

He shall teach and he shall judge.

From the ceremony of rabbinic ordination

Most newly ordained rabbis will tell you the same story when you ask what they're looking for in their first congregational posting. They'll tell you they're looking for good schools for their children's general education, a good supplemental religious school with lots of other Jewish kids, a nearby college or university where the rabbi can study or teach, and the availability of kosher food. They learn in the seminary that every congregation has more or less the same kinds of social and political dynamics; the same kinds of power struggles; and the same kinds of conflicts between founders ("veteran members," as I would come to call them) and newcomers (generally a younger generation of parents with young children).

Most of my fellow graduates were willing to go anywhere along the Eastern Seaboard. There they could remain amid the majority of American Jews and be close to the seminary and their families as well.

But I was born and bred in the Midwest and had acquired the travel bug at a very young age. Exclusively among my fellow graduates, I saw my ordination as a ticket to adventure. My goal was to become a world traveler in the tradition of Benjamin of Tudela, a twelfth-century rabbi who traveled extensively in Europe, Africa, and Asia and found a comfortable home in each Jewish community he visited. So I decided to see how far my ordination would take me.

Some months before graduation, for example, I applied for a position in Curaçao, in what was then the Netherlands Antilles, but I quickly learned they were looking for a more experienced rabbi. Longing to escape the East Coast, I next set my sights a little closer to home and turned my attention to California, thanks to the advice of Max Krieger.

I befriended fifty-six-year-old tax attorney Maxwell Krieger while serving as a student rabbi at Philadelphia's Main Line Conservative Synagogue. Max, an active member of the congregation, had just lost his beloved wife of thirty years when I began my internship. To properly mourn his loss by saying Kaddish, the daily memorial prayer recited in the presence of at least nine other fellow worshipers, Max was now a regular at the synagogue's daily morning service. He continued to attend long after the traditional end of his mourning period.

Maxwell and I hit it off from the very beginning. I got to know him quite well over time as I built up a pleasant relationship with the older gentleman. I learned he had been posted to Northern California as an army logistics officer during World War II and was clearly well traveled.

So early in my final seminary year, I asked him where he would choose to live if he could live anywhere other than Philadelphia.

Max answered, "There's a beautiful place called North Bay, California, about forty miles north of San Francisco. Today it's known as the wine country, but back during the war it was mostly cattle ranches, poultry ranches, and fruit farms. I did a lot of business for the army up there, and even though there was a war going on, they were some of the best years of my life. Idyllic years, I would say. If a good job were to open up there now, I'd go back in a heartbeat. I still have a number of Jewish friends there, and they have a small synagogue in the community too. I think today they call it the North Bay Jewish Center."

Although I had by then flown over the Atlantic many times and had lived a number of years in a foreign country, I had yet to see the Pacific Ocean, and San Francisco had continued to call to me ever since the "Summer of Love." So when the North Bay Jewish Center, the very congregation Max had mentioned, submitted a placement request to the seminary in the middle of my senior year, I jumped at the chance to apply.

After a number of back-and-forth letters and a phone conversation or two, the congregation arranged for me to make my Look, See, Decide—or LSD—trip to interview for the new position. I arrived at night and was met by a community member named Joel.

After driving north on Highway 101 for more than an hour, we exited at the south edge of town. I immediately noticed a strange yellow mist hanging over the area, illuminated by the highway lights. The air smelled like lantana mixed with seaweed, a distinctive aroma that, wafting up from the haze, provided the entire area with an eerie quality.

When a busload of Synanon commune members walked into the sanctuary that weekend for a Friday night service, I began to realize just how peculiar a place it was.

Among the active synagogue members, I found only three or four Jewish couples my age—baby boomers. A preponderant number of senior citizens inhabited the community.

Many of the congregants were tradesmen: electricians, plumbers, carpenters, house painters, and roofers. There were dairy ranchers, winemakers, vineyard managers, and egg men.

There was also a remarkable group of elderly chicken ranchers, early twentieth-century immigrants who had been lured away from San Francisco by "Hebrew Free Loans" enabling them to acquire cheap land in the North Bay area. They were imbued with the same pioneering spirit that motivated people like Gur Aryeh to leave Russia and settle on the land. And like Gur Aryeh and pioneers everywhere, North Bay men and women worked together in the early years despite the backbreaking labor.

The congregation also included one or two high school teachers and even a couple of holdover hippies. But there was nary a lawyer, doctor, or accountant among them.

It began to dawn on me during this brief LSD trip that the North Bay Jewish Center was hardly a typical late twentieth-century American Jewish congregation. And in spite of that—or because of that—I loved it!

There were some ominous signs as well. North Bay was still too small a town to attract and hold the second and third generation, so many had moved away. As the founders were now well into their senior years, it seemed to be a congregation on the verge of extinction.

In fact, it probably wouldn't have survived as an identifiable Jewish community into the late twentieth century had it not been for the completion of Highway 101. The new road brought North Bay within an easy commute of San Francisco, fueling a housing boom. As a result, small five-acre chicken ranchers rushed to build spec houses on their property, transforming themselves into wealthy developers virtually overnight. The highway also brought a small group of young "mainstream" American Jewish families looking for affordable housing within San Francisco's orbit. These baby boomers soon reshaped this most unconventional Jewish congregation—housed in a small stucco building along a side street near downtown—into what might have been considered a "nearly normative" small-town congregation.

The congregation called itself "conservative" but chose not to affiliate with the national Conservative Jewish movement, headquartered in New York, chiefly because the congregation's leaders couldn't see any advantage in affiliating with such a far-off, big-city organization.

One could safely say the founders of the North Bay Jewish Center subscribed wholeheartedly to my sardonic depiction of the differences between the three major American Jewish movements: Orthodox, Conservative, and Reform.

"Three men are lying on a bed," I liked to jest, relating an anecdote in the name of my father, Louis. "Orthodox on the right, Conservative in the middle, and Reform on the left. The man on the right pulls the blanket his way, the man on the left pulls the blanket back the other way, but the guy in the middle always gets covered."

"Yep, that's us," said NBJC president Bob Plitman, apparently unperturbed by the light jab. "That way, we cover all the bases. We aspire to be—how do you say it back east? Inclusive!"

Despite my misgivings, I returned to Philadelphia to complete my studies and consider the employment opportunity. I had a few more back-and-forth discussions with the NBJC. In the end, I decided—along with my wife, Linda (a California native who liked to point with pride to the fact that she was a *real* Californian, "not one of those transplants from back east") and our young daughter, Rachel—to accept the offer of the "nearly normative" congregation.

"It must be the most eclectic gathering of Hebrews the Western world has ever seen," I told Linda after that first visit. "So far off the grid and yet so compelling a challenge!" That thought would stay with me throughout my twenty-year career in North Bay.

I can humbly say I brought a number of innovations to the new congregation, and at least a few of them were well received. But this semirural community was slow to adapt to what were, on the East Coast, already well-established norms among the more liberal, non-Orthodox congregations. Chief among the innovations, of course, was the notion of complete spiritual equality for women.

Religion is conservative by its very nature, and traditional Judaism is no exception. One of the leaders of the premodern European Orthodox Jewish community, in fact, famously proclaimed, "Anything new is forbidden by the Torah," putting an end to what had been, up to that stage, the natural evolution of Jewish practice. That we still see today some Jews dressed in the black garb, fur hats, long kaftans, and white leggings of seventeenth-century Polish noblemen—what I like to call the Hollywood image of a Jew—is a case in point. Religion tends to get stuck in the past.

So it was no surprise that even in the late twentieth century, Orthodox Jewish women remained in their traditional roles of housewives and mothers, apparently content to be seated in a separate section in the synagogue, forbidden to raise their voices in song "so as not to entice the menfolk and fill their minds with wanton desires."

I was relieved to find mixed-gender seating at North Bay, at least. But because some of the founders of the North Bay Jewish Center had been raised in an Orthodox environment, they were reluctant to call a woman up to the Torah, for example, or allow a woman to become president of the synagogue. "This women's lib thing is just a fad," they argued, and since virtually all newcomers courteously deferred to the wishes of the veteran founders, nothing changed.

But I wasn't afraid to push the boundaries. I began to prepare the path to change by preaching and teaching about the role of women in Judaism. I made reference to the fact that there had been many prominent Jewish women in the past, that some of them actually taught Torah in mixed company, that the first woman rabbi had already been ordained way back in 1935 ("She was Reform," the opposition countered), that the movement for women's equality was no more a fad than the civil rights movement of the 1960s. But the entrenched leadership would not budge on the issue.

When, on July 12, 1984, Democratic presidential candidate Walter Mondale selected Geraldine Ferraro as his vice-presidential running mate, I decided to make my move. The very next Saturday, after a bit of clandestine planning, I called Heather Tuchman up to the Torah. An audible gasp arose from the congregation as Heather recited her blessings as clearly and fluently as any male NBJC member. One or two of the "veterans" stalked out of the sanctuary.

Heather, having completed her honor and been blessed by the rabbi, turned to the seated members and said, "It's about time."

Six months later, she was elected president of the North Bay Jewish Center by a two-to-one margin.

CHAPTER XV.

 NORTH BAY. 1978–98.

How cramped becomes a spacious land where two enemies try to stand,
just as in a tiny bit of space there's room enough where friends embrace.

RABBI JUDAH AL-HARIZI

My twenty years as the rabbi of North Bay, California, were characterized by some profound developments in the American Jewish community. These developments came in response to earlier global events that had a deep effect on American Jews. Two of these events, in fact—the Holocaust and the birth of Israel—were considered so significant that a prominent twentieth-century scholar, Professor Emil Fackenheim of the University of Toronto, called them "Sinai events." He meant that the two events transformed the lives of Jews as profoundly as the events at Mount Sinai, when the newly liberated Israelite slaves stood at the foot of the mountain and received the Ten Commandments.

In the 1980s and '90s, the American Jewish community grew in stature and influence not seen since the early Middle Ages, during the "golden age" of Spanish Jewry. In the final decades of the twentieth century, Jewish culture became a main thread in the American tapestry. The kosher food industry, for example, grew to a multibillion-dollar enterprise; American Jews, a tiny percentage of the American population, were clearly not the only customers. Words like *chutzpah, kibitz, kosher, schlep,* and *schmooze* became part of the American vernacular along with some more humorous earthy words of derogation. Hanukkah joined Christmas as a major winter holiday. University doors and corporate doors that were once closed now opened. A Jewish senator became his party's candidate for vice president, while a number of other Jews were elected to Congress. Jews became governors of significant electoral states. One had already served as secretary of state, while still others held significant posts in the State Department. Jewish journalists were everywhere to be seen and heard.

Between 1980 and 2000, which roughly coincided with my twenty years at NBJC, the Holocaust—through print media, theater performances, movies, museum exhibitions, and the gradual willingness of traumatized survivors to speak out—was so widely studied that it became a vital part of the public school curriculum throughout America. The same period saw the burgeoning of Jewish studies departments in virtually every major American university, featuring courses in Hebrew, Bible, Talmud, Jewish history, and modern Jewish literature, among others.

Because of the Holocaust and the creation of Israel, the world Jewish community underwent a sea change in the late twentieth century. That sea change was also swept in by something I never thought I would see in my lifetime. On March 26, 1979, an exceptionally brave man, the president of Egypt, Anwar Sadat, shook hands with Israel's prime minister, Menachem Begin, on the White House lawn while the whole world looked on with great anticipation. For a brief while, an air of optimism hung over the entire region. Sadat went so far as to make a historic journey to Jerusalem, where he addressed the Knesset and spoke to the world about peace.

We were all like dreamers until the terrible day when Sadat was assassinated by extremists within his own army in 1981. But Israel nevertheless completed its negotiated withdrawal from the Sinai Peninsula, and Egypt too continued to uphold its end of the bargain. And the peace treaty between the two former enemies still holds to this day.

The State of Israel too developed in many ways during the late twentieth century, becoming a dominant power in the Middle East, a seedbed of technological advances in the agricultural, military, communications, and medical research fields. In the days of my earlier sojourn, the population of that tiny country barely reached three million. By 1998, it had more than doubled. And because of its impressive international accomplishments, Israel grew during that period from being an underdog in the Six-Day War to a bastion of democracy in the Middle East, a vital ally of the United States, with a flourishing economy and the strongest military in the region.

We members of the North Bay Jewish Center, in a most humble way in our little corner of the world, were pleased to play a small part in these global developments. As the local spokesman for my community, for example, I began to be called upon to speak about Judaism in a number of public school settings. I also became a frequent presenter at nearby North Bay University, sometimes in conjunction with clergymen and clergywomen of other faiths, but often alone. We inaugurated an annual interfaith Thanksgiving service with nearby Summit Presbyterian Church as well as an annual countywide Holocaust commemoration in conjunction with the university.

In our growing Jewish center, meanwhile, the 1980s also saw the introduction of a number of new synagogue programs, among them the "Shabbat Seder," a monthly Friday-evening experience modeled on that most widely observed of all Jewish festivals, the Passover Seder.

Our Shabbat Seder featured many of the forms, if not the content, of the typical Passover Seder: songs, blessings, table rituals, dialogue, and a festive meal. In addition, we blended in important elements of the regular Friday-evening Shabbat worship service: some Sabbath prayers and a brief topical sermon or, if children were present, a story.

One particular Friday evening after the famous White House lawn handshake, I told the story about the threshing floor of Aravna the Jebusite, as recorded in the Second Book of Samuel. In the text, King David is instructed to purchase the threshing floor on the top of a mountain in Jerusalem and, as recorded in chapter 24, verse 21, "set up there an altar to the Lord." According to tradition, the altar on that spot became the centerpiece of the both the First and Second Temples that would eventually occupy the site. The mount, called Haram al-Sharif by Muslims and the Temple Mount by Jews, is considered sacred by all three great monotheistic religions to this day.

"Why was this particular site, Aravna's threshing floor, chosen?" I asked the Shabbat Seder gathering that Friday evening. "First of all, most likely for its geographic prominence. It's high on a Jerusalem hill, visible from all directions. But our tradition teaches that God chose the site for a more transcendent reason, as this story illustrates:

> Aravna and his younger brother inherited the mount from their father, but the brothers soon quarreled. So they divided the territory between them and built a fence down the middle. Each quarreling brother planted a wheat field on his respective side of the fence. Aravna, the eldest, was married at the time and had two children. His brother was a bachelor. The years went by, but the brothers never spoke to each other.
>
> After some time, Aravna, the married brother, said to himself, "I have a wife and a son and a daughter to help me with the wheat harvest, but my brother has no one." So, in the middle of the night, he gathered up a bundle of wheat, walked up to the fence and lowered the bundle onto his brother's side.
>
> The next morning, upon seeing the bundle on his side, Aravna's brother said, "What is this? Could it be a gift from my brother? But he has four mouths to feed, and I have only one." So he placed the bundle back on Aravna's side of the fence and added a second bundle from his own crop.
>
> The next morning, the younger brother found three bundles on his side, and the following morning, after giving four back, five.
>
> After seven such days of back-and-forth giving, the bachelor brother went out to the fence in the middle of the night, where he found Aravna

lowering bundle after bundle of wheat over the fence. The younger brother proceeded to cut a big hole in the fence. The two brothers met in the middle, hugged each other warmly, and talked together well past sunrise.

When God looked down upon the two brothers embracing in the middle of that mountain field, he said to his ministering angels, "This is where my temple shall be built." So God told King David to purchase the site and said, "My temple shall be a house of prayer for all people."

"Now," I concluded, "if the two brothers could put aside their differences for the sake of peace, shouldn't we and our Muslim brothers be able to set aside our differences and embrace one another on the very same Temple Mount?"

When the Shabbat Seder was over, an active congregant, sixty-eight-year-old Harry Estrin, introduced me to his own brother, who had come into town from Boston for a visit.

While people were filtering out of the social hall, Harry motioned to me and said quietly, "Rabbi, come here with us, please."

The three of us walked into a corner of the room.

"How did you know? Only our families know," he whispered to me in the presence of his brother.

"Know what?" I asked.

"That my brother and I haven't talked in thirty years. That we finally agreed to let go of the past and we're together this weekend for the first time in more than three decades. How did you know?"

I didn't know, of course. I had no idea. But a wise old rabbi once told me that what some people call "coincidence" is only God working his way anonymously in the world.

CHAPTER XVI.

✈ NORTH BAY. 1982–83.

Do not look only at the outward appearance
but consider what is within.

<small>Pirkei Avot: Sayings of the Fathers, chapter iv</small>

"How long has it been since you left Israel, Rabbi?" Bob Plitman asked me at the end of the fall High Holy Days in my fourth year with the congregation.

"Eight years," I answered, "but it feels like longer." I knew Bob well enough by now to know he had something up his sleeve.

"We'd like to help you get back there. Because you know the country so well, why don't you think about organizing a Holy Land tour? I'll support you if you do. We might even think about a spot on the air."

Plitman—owner of North Bay's radio station KGNB and still president of the congregation at the time—was newly married to Janice Barkan, a native of Canada. Janice was in the process of setting up her own travel agency, North Bay Travel Adventures. While she planned to specialize in travel to Mexico, Costa Rica, and Hawaii, Bob evidently thought the idea of a group tour to Israel might give her a chance to branch out a bit.

His idea fell upon fertile soil. Since leaving Israel, I had often dreamed of organizing such a trip. I felt that much of my teaching about modern Jewish history could come alive with an educational tour of the Holy Land. After all, it had worked for *me* during my sojourn on Kibbutz Haziv. Maybe now I could "share the experience" with others in true California style.

"Great idea," I answered the president with unmasked enthusiasm. "You know, I was born around the same time as the State of Israel. I'd love to celebrate 'our' thirty-fifth birthday together. I'd suggest late April, next spring. The weather is usually moderate, the flowers are in full bloom, and the Easter and Passover crowds will have gone home. Let's go then!"

When eighteen people indicated an interest in the tour, I suggested we hold three orientation seminars prior to the pilgrimage. The classes, I hoped, would help build camaraderie, foster a sense of group identity, and give participants a deeper understanding of the history of the Holy Land. So Janice Plitman produced a four-color brochure and labeled the orientation seminar series, "Layers of Civilization Beneath the Soil of Israel."

Three weeks before the scheduled departure, President Plitman came into my office. "Rabbi, there's something we need to discuss," he told me in a rather serious tone.

"Sure, Bob." I tried to put on a happy face despite my trepidation.

"Rabbi, you know you are our first full-time rabbi. In the past, for most of this congregation's life, we just had rabbis who drove up from San Francisco or Oakland to take care of our immediate needs—you know, weddings and funerals and such. Only in the early sixties were we able to afford someone to visit on regular weekends and holidays. And only later after that did we have enough to pay for someone to come up an additional two weekdays each week to run our religious school."

I knew all that and wondered where he was going with the history lesson.

"So, we've never had a full-time resident rabbi," Plitman continued. "At least, not until you came along. Now don't get me wrong. You're doing a great job. But some of the executive committee members are a bit perturbed that you're leading this tour to Israel—a place none of them have been—and you're expecting to count it as work time, not vacation time."

Oh, boy, I thought to myself. *This really is a small town.*

But thank God, I held my feelings in check and said only, "But Bob, aren't you the one who urged me to do this?"

"Yes, I was. I mean, I am. That's why I argued in your favor. I know you've put in a lot of extra time on the project already. And you will work hard during the tour. So I convinced them to compromise, and I hope you'll accept our suggestion. We were able to come up with this: you'll be gone for sixteen days. How about if you take one week—less than one-half the time—as vacation and the rest as your contracted work time? That's the best I could get."

There was a long pause in our conversation as I mulled over the proposition, trying to look at it from their point of view. A trip to Israel would be a vacation for them, so why not for me? They were, after all, willing to compromise, and that was probably the most important thing.

With as much tactfulness as I could muster, I said, "Sure, Bob. We'll deduct one week from my annual vacation allotment. Thanks for your hard work." And that was that.

After months of preparation, the eighteen pilgrims and I, their rabbi-cum-tour-organizer, made the short hop to LA on a commuter airline and boarded the El Al plane. As I took my seat, I was glad I had made a special request with Janice when she first booked the tickets.

"Please seat me out of sight as much as possible," I had told her. "As many as ten or twelve rows behind the group. That way, I can keep an eye on them but get some rest before the real twenty-four-seven work begins. Besides, with the blue-and-white colors of Israel, Hebrew-speaking stewards and stewardesses, and a menu featuring pita and hummus, their trip to Israel will actually begin the moment they board. Let the El Al crew take over for a while."

On the day of departure, I took my back-of-the cabin seat next to a San Franciscan woman who appeared to be about fiftysomething, which seemed old to me at the time. (It's amusing how one's perspective changes as the years pass.)

After the customary introductions, she blurted out, "I can't wait to see those El Al stewards walking up and down these aisles. My friends tell me they're real hunks."

She was absolutely right, of course. The young uniformed men of Israel were attractive—no one could argue with that.

In fact, I had touted the very same notion to the potential pilgrims, promising, "You'll see the army wherever you go, and you'll probably agree with the consensus that the Israel Defense Force, or IDF, is the handsomest army in the world." I must have sounded a bit like a salesman, but I was convinced that if I appealed to the women, their husbands might come along too. It worked.

We flew twelve hours before landing in Rome for a brief stopover, but I had a difficult time sleeping. Midflight, I got up to get a drink of water in the galley. There I was met by one of the stewards, a thin, dark-haired young man with whom I conversed in Hebrew.

"Where are you from?" the steward inquired. Safe conversation opener.

"A small town not far from San Francisco," I replied.

The steward's eyes lit up.

"Ah," he said somewhat wistfully in Hebrew, "San Francisco. *Yesh shama harbey alizim.*"

I understood most of the statement. He said, "There are many *alizim* there," but I didn't quite grasp the meaning of the term *alizim*. My fourteen-year-old Herzl Camp girlfriend, Aliza Lewin, once told me her name meant "joyful," so I guessed *alizim* might be the plural form of the same word.

After a moment of puzzlement, I became convinced the steward was referring to the stereotype about San Franciscans: easygoing, playful, lighthearted folks, gleefully "tripping out" on the streets of a post-hippie paradise.

"*Ken, ken*," I responded in his native tongue. "San Francisco is full of cheerful, happy, joyous people." I used every Hebrew synonym I knew for *joyful*.

"*Lo, lo.*" The steward grew intense. "*Hitkavanti alizim.*" That is, "I meant *alizim*."

And then, leaning a little closer and peering into my eyes, he repeated the term and translated it in the same breath, with some noticeable emphasis: "*Alizim.* Gay."

"Oh," I said, feeling stupid for not catching the steward's drift.

Not wanting to end the conversation on an awkward note, I reluctantly agreed with the steward's characterization of San Franciscans, another common stereotype. "*Ken, ken. Yesh shama harbey alizim.*" Or, "Yes, yes. There *are* many gay people there."

I stepped back against the wall of the narrow galley to open a little more space between us. But I was completely taken aback by what came next. He leaned even closer and peered even more intently into my eyes.

"*Zeh nosay m'od karov aylai*," he said very earnestly. Meaning, "That is a subject that is very close to me."

I must admit, reflecting upon it now, that his approach was not at all aggressive. But the entire encounter was getting a bit *too close* for my comfort. I'm not particularly adept at thinking quickly on my feet. I'm more likely, rather, to mull over a conversation in my mind—telling myself over and over again, *I should have said this, I should have done that*—well after the opportune moment had already long passed.

But this time, my mind went into high gear. In an instant, I drew my wallet out of my back pocket and opened it to a photo of my wife, Linda; our daughter, Rachel; and our three-year-old son, David.

I replied slowly and carefully with a version of the steward's own words: "*Zeh nosay* lo *karov aylai.*" Or, "That is a subject that is *not* very close to me."

I hoped I had met his gentle approach with an equally mild brush-off. I then smiled deferentially, turned down the aisle, and sauntered back to my seat.

When I found the woman in the seat next to me also awake, I whispered to her, "I just had a very interesting conversation with one of your El Al hunks."

I ended up leading two more congregational tours to Israel—one every five years during the first fifteen years of my twenty-year tenure. Each tour was timed to coincide with Israel's annual Independence Day celebrations, milestones which happily coincided with significant events in my own life—namely, my thirty-fifth, fortieth, and forty-fifth birthdays. I always considered it providential to have been born the same year in the same season as the State of Israel.

And each subsequent group tour, of course, included a week of my vacation time. As Linda liked to explain, it was all done in accordance with the golden rule, which is, "Whoever has the gold makes the rules." But at least they were willing to compromise.

The fortieth anniversary tour was the trickiest one. The first Palestinian intifada uprising broke out in December 1987 when an Israeli army truck accidentally crushed a car in a Palestinian refugee camp, killing its four occupants. The uprising that ensued began nonviolently but soon escalated. Nevertheless, I began to advertise the "Israel Fortieth Anniversary Pilgrimage" in January.

When one of NBJC's prominent members asked me, "How can you go there now?" I presented my response in a sermon.

"How can we *not* go?" I argued. "When a member of your family is in trouble, do you stay where you are? Or do you reach out to them, go to them, put your arms around them, and comfort them to demonstrate your support?"

Because the intifada was having a deleterious effect on tourism, this fortieth anniversary pilgrimage, ironically, turned out to be the best by almost every measure. The number of participants was surprisingly up, the prices were down, participant satisfaction was palpable, and the Israeli tourism community proved exceptionally gracious and grateful that we had bothered to come.

Nevertheless, there was a changed dynamic on the ground, especially in Jerusalem. In 1983, on my first group tour, anyone could wander freely through the Old City of Jerusalem as well as throughout the Arab neighborhoods of East Jerusalem beyond the Old City walls.

In fact, during the first tour in 1983, I acted on a tip from a friend and visited a particular pottery shop in Arab East Jerusalem, not far from the American consulate. There at the shop I ordered a gorgeous three-inch-by-seven-inch painted terra-cotta address tile with my family name calligraphically inscribed in Hebrew, Arabic, and English, all attractively embellished with Middle Eastern artistic motifs. Every tile in the shop was unique, a real work of art, yet they could be acquired for the unbelievably low price of five US dollars per tile. The shop owner assured me my tile would be ready for pickup in ten days, and he turned out to be a man of his word.

So, at our final orientation session before departing in the spring of 1988, I promised my group they wouldn't have to shop around for souvenir gifts to bring back to their loved ones. I showed them the tile I had purchased in 1983 and asked them to think about whose names they would want written on their tiles. I said it would be the perfect souvenir for their own households as well as exquisite gifts for their friends and loved ones.

The plan was for me to travel up to Jerusalem alone the day after our arrival in Tel Aviv and place the orders. Jerusalem would be the final destination of our fourteen-day tour, and I would collect the finished tiles in ten days and deliver them to each person.

On the first day of the pilgrimage to the Holy Land, the group toured Tel Aviv under the direction of a licensed guide while I took the public bus up to Jerusalem with their orders in hand.

But this was not 1983. This was 1988, and the first intifada uprising was in full swing. Much had changed in five years. Strangers strolling in East Jerusalem were now taking their lives in their own hands. Not being aware of this change was a serious miscalculation.

Stepping just outside Damascus Gate in East Jerusalem, I was immediately surrounded by young Arab men. They came out of nowhere, and suddenly I was surrounded on all sides. It was a threatening situation, and I was quite frightened. I thought, *Maybe they think I'm Israeli.* I guess I somewhat looked the part.

So I said to them in my clear midwestern English, "I'm looking for the American consulate."

When they realized I was American, they backed off. One of them pointed me in the direction of the consulate, which, of course, I already knew.

I eventually made it to the pottery shop, only to find out the situation there had also changed considerably in five years. I soon learned I had become a victim of the pottery shop's success. Address tiles were popular in the 1980s, appearing at the entryways of hundreds of American homes. Many of them emanated from this unique shop in East Jerusalem. Overwhelmed with customers from around the world, the owner could no longer promise to fill an order within ten days. It would take four weeks.

"I'll send them to you in the post," the busy owner said, gesturing toward the shelves behind him filled with piles of completed tiles waiting to be shipped. "You'll get them sometime next month."

"But I promised these people. They've come all the way from America for your beautiful artwork," I pleaded, hoping the flattery would convince him to make an exception.

"America!" the shopkeeper answered dismissively, raising his voice. "We have orders here from Japan, even from Australia! Here, look. You can see how busy we are."

The owner was growing impatient now as he pulled me to the doorway so I could see the busy workroom, then he roughly escorted me back to my side of the counter.

"I'll send them to you," he said. "You'll get them in a month. Don't worry. It will be okay."

But I knew it would not be okay. I could see exactly how the tiles were being wrapped in simple brown paper, one on top of the other, with no cushioning between them. Bubble Wrap had, evidently, not yet been introduced to East Jerusalem.

I was all too aware of the high probability that the fragile tiles would never make it to their destinations intact, if they made it at all. Some of them would certainly break in transit, when the shop owner would no longer be liable. The idea of insured delivery was then unknown in the Middle East. Probably still is.

I watched the owner busily addressing a package of five tiles piled one on top of another. As I casually glanced down at the name of the addressee, I could hardly believe what I saw. This particular package, at this very moment as I stood at the counter in this East Jerusalem shop, was going to—could this be?—my mother's first cousin in San Jose! Dr. Arthur Rubin—who, unbeknownst to me, had been in Israel for Passover just a month before—had evidently ordered tiles as gifts for the five nurses on his staff at San Jose General Hospital!

"This is amazing!" I cried out, pointing to the package as the shopkeeper completed the address label. "That package is going to my cousin in San Jose!"

And yet once again, I suddenly found myself thinking quickly on my feet.

"If you complete my order by the time I return to Jerusalem in ten days," I now bargained with the shop owner, "I will personally deliver these tiles to my cousin in San Jose."

The deal was sealed. By the skin of my teeth—*was it divine providence?*—I fulfilled my orientation promise and kept my reputation intact. On our final full day in Jerusalem, we gathered in the hotel lobby to distribute the terra-cotta address tiles.

I couldn't sleep that night—the night before our departure. We had chosen the hotel chiefly for its location. It was close to the Old City at the edge of west Jerusalem, about a fifteen-minute walk from the Western Wall. I got dressed at around midnight and walked toward the Wall to insert a prayer into a crevice between the stones, something I hadn't had a chance to do during our very busy tour.

When I approached the Wall plaza a little after midnight, I found it eerily empty. At most other times, throngs of people—tourists, residents, guides, and guards—filled every square meter. As I walked slowly toward the Wall, I noticed one person—an old man dressed in flowing white robes with a long white beard and a kind of turban on his head. He was watching me from beneath the archway at the northeast corner of the Wall. I nodded in his direction, placed my prayer in a crack between two huge stones, and stood leaning against the Wall with both hands, uttering a short prayer.

When I turned from the Wall, the man was standing a few feet behind me. He said to me in a kind, gentle Hebrew voice, "Would you like me to bless you?"

I reached into my pocket to confirm I had some money, as I knew the custom in most holy places was to receive a blessing and then give a small donation.

Facing the man, I bowed my head as he placed both his hands on my head. He said a few words I didn't understand, and then he uttered the Priestly Benediction, the most widely known blessing from the Hebrew Bible:

May the Lord bless you and watch over you; may God cause his light to shine upon you and be gracious unto you; may the Holy One bestow favor upon you and grant you peace.

As he spoke the words, a palpable bolt of energy rushed through my body.

I lifted my head, said thank you to the man, and reached back into my pocket to give him the monetary gift.

But to my surprise, he held his hand up to indicate no and said, "God's blessing is a gift to you. May you be blessed on all your journeys."

An old rabbi once said that the air of the Land of Israel makes one wise. I don't know about wisdom. But I can attest that even before we boarded the El Al plane for our return flight a few hours later, I was already floating on that air.

On the way home, I realized I could safely allow myself to fall in love again with the Land of Israel. But from now on, I would come only as a tourist.

CHAPTER XVII.

 NORTH BAY. 1997–98.

Let your memory be your travel bag.

ALEKSANDR SOLZHENITSYN

When I reached the beginning of my fiftieth year of life, my daughter, Rachel, was finishing her junior year in college and my son, David, was in his junior year in high school. So as two potential empty nesters, Linda and I decided to explore the idea of serving abroad.

There was no doubt I still had a case of *shpilkes*, a kind of perpetual kinetic energy, the inability to stay in one place for too long. The fact that I had remained in North Bay nearly twenty years was a record for me, the longest I had stayed in one place my entire life, but now I was growing restless. I had gone into the rabbinate with the personal goal of contributing to the creative survival of the Jewish people, and after two decades of service, I felt I had, in a very modest and humble way, accomplished that mission. But I still had the travel bug and was ready for something new.

So in the autumn of 1997, just after the High Holy Days, I drew Raymond Pamone aside for a private chat. Ray, an active member of the congregation, had served in the US Merchant Marine and had visited just about every friendly port in the world.

I sidled up to him one day after services and asked, "Ray, you've been just about everywhere on the planet. What, in your opinion, is the most beautiful country on earth?"

I really thought Ray would have to take some time to consider his answer, but to my surprise, it came out right away.

"New Zealand," Ray replied, hardly skipping a beat. "Without a doubt, the most beautiful country in this whole wide world is New Zealand."

"Why do you say that?" I asked.

"Because it's really a microcosm of some of this blessed earth's most gorgeous places. In New Zealand, you can find the wine country of Northern California, the islands of Puget Sound, the geysers of Yellowstone, the fjords of Norway, the Alps of Switzerland, and the glaciers of Alaska—to say nothing of hundreds of miles of exquisite coastline with seals and whales and dolphins and exotic birds everywhere to be seen. And it's all rolled up into two islands that can each be traversed, north to south, in about eight hours, though that's something you'd never want to do! You'd want to take your time exploring all the coves and inlets, the byways and the highways, and the gorgeous walking tracks. And it's relatively uncrowded as well, with a total population of only four million people. Hey"—he paused a moment in his rhapsodic account—"I ought to go work for their tourist board! But," he added in a tone of sincerity, "none of this is hype."

That's all it took. I was sold. Soon Rachel would be happily ensconced in a job in San Francisco, and David enrolled at my own alma mater, the University of Michigan. It was clearly time for a transition.

Besides, the congregation had grown too large for one rabbi to handle, but the board was reluctant to hire an assistant rabbi to help me manage. They had embarked upon an expansion program and wished to concentrate their energies on building a new school wing rather than devote so large a percentage of their budget to "personnel," as they liked to describe a rabbi's role in the organization. In my opinion, they had developed a classic case of an "edifice complex" by putting their faith in buildings and grounds rather than in staff and programming.

So Ray's glowing description, my children's decision to scatter, the congregation's fiscal philosophy, my twenty years of service, and my upcoming fiftieth birthday all conspired to help me make up my mind to look elsewhere. If successful, of course, I would give ample notice so as to enable the congregation to find a younger, more energetic, and—how would they say it?—*less expensive* rabbi to take over.

It's not as if the twenty years had been uneventful, however. Far from it. I often reflected with fondness upon the many volunteers who served the community nobly and quietly while shunning the limelight. I chuckle at the singular memory of the Hebrew-school teacher who pulled into the synagogue parking lot one cold winter's morning with a Christmas tree tied to the roof of her car. I enjoy the fact that I stayed long enough to conduct a number of naming services for babies born into the community, then officiate at Bar Mitzvah ceremonies for the same children thirteen years later, and ultimately speak at graduation exercises upon the completion of their high school years. Had I stayed longer, I might have been asked to conduct a wedding ceremony or two for the same children-turned-adults, but that was not to be.

Being a rabbi opened up a number of other doors for me. I once shared the dais, for example, with a president of the United

States. Well, actually, Gerald Ford was a former president at the time, but I look back upon that experience as a great moment. And when NBJC member Richard Catlin was elected commodore of the North Bay Harbor Yacht Club, he called upon me on more than one occasion to bless the fleet and rewarded me with free sailing lessons.

And after Baron Philippe de Rothschild, a Jewish Frenchman, partnered with Robert Mondavi, a Catholic Californian, to create Opus One winery, I, along with a local Catholic priest, was often called to bless their annual grape harvest. Both congregations built quite an inventory of premium wines from the in-kind gratuities we received. In fact, following our tour to Israel in 1993, I mixed some of the soil of Israel with the soil of an Opus One vineyard as part of a ceremony. The vineyard manager told me the next year's crop was particularly robust, but to this day, I'm not sure if he was having me on or not.

Over the twenty years of service, I was privileged to meet a number of prominent scholars and writers and was often interviewed on local television and radio. I established an "elderseminar" program and experienced the joys of designing and leading Jewish heritage tours to pioneering California sites as well as to Europe and Israel. When the Soviet Union collapsed, I was fortunate to be one of the first rabbis invited to visit the new FSU, or former Soviet Union.

I was also proud of the preschool I founded and recall the satisfaction I felt when the synagogue's neglected backyard was transformed into a school playground.

And of course, there was the growth of the congregation to reflect upon—a doubling in the first ten years and another 50 percent growth over the next decade, a rate that paralleled the growth of the entire city of North Bay.

Though by the end of my twenty-year stay, almost all the founding members of the North Bay Jewish Center had either passed away or were seriously ill. I'm sad to think about that now. I loved conducting weddings, but I hated funerals and was by then officiating at far too many of them.

But whenever I reflect upon my years at NBJC, one incident from that entire period stands out from all the rest.

It began with a phone call. It was 1991.

"Hello, Rabbi Kadison. This is Bassem ibn Talal. I teach in the criminal justice department at North Bay State University."

"Yes?" I replied somewhat tentatively, telling myself, *This will be interesting.*

"I was in the audience when you came to speak at the world religions forum some months ago. You may remember that I asked a somewhat provocative question about peace in the Middle East."

The Arabic accent on the other end of the line was stimulating my memory—as well as a generous amount of apprehension. North Bay State wasn't large enough to support a Jewish studies or even a more general religious studies program, but I had been a frequent lecturer on campus. Arab students often attended my lectures, and I tried to field their challenging questions as deftly as I could.

"Ah, yes, I think I do remember you, Mr. . . . . ah . . . Talal."

"Bassem," he quickly replied.

"Yes, thank you, Bassem. You're from Saudi Arabia, if I remember correctly. We chatted for a bit after the forum." I am blessed with a good memory, especially when it comes to people and my interactions with them.

"Yes, that's right. But I'm from Dubai, United Arab Emirates, actually. I remember your answer quite well. When I asked whether you thought peace was possible given right-wing intransigence in Israel, you said it took a conservative Republican in America to make peace with Communist China, just as it took right-wing Israeli prime minister Menachem Begin to make peace with Egypt. You said you had never thought you would see peace between Israel and *any* of its neighbors in your lifetime, yet here we are with a long-lasting peace agreement between Israel and Egypt and an even warmer peace between Jordan and Israel. I liked your answer."

It sounded as though Bassem had a good memory too.

"Thank you, Bassem. And how can I help you now?" I asked, letting my guard down a little—but only a small little.

"Well, Rabbi, it's a bit of a long story. I'm writing my master's thesis here at North Bay State on extremist groups in North America, and I've just heard that the West Coast Nazi Party is planning an event right here in North Bay County. Have you heard about their plans?"

There was a long silence on my end of the line. *Is he trying to provoke me?* I wondered for a moment. Then I remembered the Talmud's admonition, "Judge every man on the scale of merit," which I understood to mean, "Give them the benefit of the doubt." I softened.

"No, Bassem. This is the first I've heard of it. Please tell me what you know."

"Well, they're calling it an 'Aryan Woodstock.' I guess they're inviting some 'biker bands,' as one might call them, to perform.

They hope to attract a large young crowd to make a sort of pro-Nazi rally out of it. They should come out with a flyer any day now."

"Oy," came my unfiltered response, followed by another silence.

"So, Rabbi, as part of my research, I would like to come and interview you about the subject, to gauge the Jewish community's response."

I was impressed by Bassem's command of English, and I appreciated the fact that his words seemed sincere.

"When are they planning this Woodstock thing?" I inquired.

"Well, according to my information, they've scheduled it for some Saturday next month. So, do you think we can talk next Thursday afternoon?"

"Yes, certainly. Let me put you on the line with Nancy, my secretary, to find a convenient time. *Ma'a salama*, Bassem."

Bad news, but thanks for the genuine heads-up, I added to myself.

"*Shalom*, Rabbi Kadison, and thank you very much."

Immediately, I got on the phone to Frank Grey, president of the North Bay Ministerial Association. I was serving as the association's secretary at the time and had developed a cordial relationship of mutual respect with Reverend Grey, the town's preeminent cleric and head of Summit Presbyterian Church.

I skipped the customary pleasantries. "Frank, have you heard about a Nazi rally? I just got off the phone with someone from the criminal justice department at North Bay State."

"A blight on our community, that's for sure," came Reverend Grey's calm reply. "I just found out this morning. Did you know they're planning it on Hitler's birthday, April 20?"

"Good heavens!" I cried out. "I've got a Bar Mitzvah here that morning."

After a long silence, during which I felt I could actually hear the wheels of Frank Grey's mind churning, the good reverend spoke up. "Jonathan, I think I know what we can do. What's your seating capacity?"

"Well, we can open up the social hall and put out folding chairs, so I would say four hundred or so. Why?"

Frank was lost in thought again. "Jonathan," he finally said, "will you ask the Bar Mitzvah family if they can handle a capacity crowd? Just for the service—we won't stay for the social hour afterward. And can you ask them if they'd mind if I spoke for a brief moment at the service? I know *you* won't mind, will you? After all, you owe me one. Last time you spoke at my church, I told you ten minutes max, and you spoke for twenty!"

We both chuckled at the reference. Then Frank, ever the diplomat, continued, "I'm just kibitzing you, of course, Jonathan. But let's work together to turn this thing into a positive experience for the whole community."

I had developed a great deal of confidence in Frank Grey's leadership over the years, so I readily agreed to do whatever he had in mind, however vague it seemed at the moment.

"Just one more thing before I let you go, Jonathan. I'm calling an emergency meeting of the ministerial association for next Thursday morning. I hope to have the chief of police on hand to strategize with us."

"Right. *Shalom*, Frank."

"And peace be with you too, my friend. And don't worry. After all, didn't the biblical Mordecai say to Esther something like, 'Who knows but that you have come to your position for just such a time as this'?"

"Oy," I muttered yet again.

My good friend Frank Grey, on the other hand, was laughing convulsively as he hung up the phone.

During our private meeting the following Thursday afternoon, Bassem ibn Talal revealed in confidence something even the chief of police apparently did not know: Donald Miles, deputy führer of the West Coast Nazi Party—an army veteran with a prison record whose name appeared on every Aryan Woodstock pamphlet— was, in fact, Jewish.

"He grew up in Albuquerque," Bassem explained. "His father was Jewish, and the mother, born Catholic, converted to Judaism before the boy was born. Here's a copy in the synagogue registry that shows Donald became a Bar Mitzvah at Temple Isaiah in 1971. You are welcome to do with this what you wish."

"This is so bizarre," I said, shaking my head in disbelief.

"There's more," Bassem continued. "Evidently, sometime after the Bar Mitzvah, the father divorced the mother and showed no interest in having anything to do with either her or Donald, though he was forced by the court to pay alimony and child support before the mother remarried. The mom not only renounced her conversion but also became a raging anti-Semite. Donald evidently bought into her worldview and then went off to join the army. During one of his furloughs, he conspired to murder the dad and wound up at the Los Lunas prison, where he served five years. That's how I came to learn about him.

"Donald Miles doesn't know that I know anything about his background, and I don't want anyone to know what I've told you because I need unfettered access to his group for my research. I'm studying them, but I have no particular love for them. I'm sharing this information with you in utmost confidence because I trust you'll know how to manage the information for its greatest effect."

On a rainy Saturday, April 20, 1991, hundreds of Bay Area protestors, some from as far away as San Jose, gathered just outside the gate of the hilltop ranch the West Coast Nazi Party had rented for the day. The protestors brought drums, trumpets, and various crude instruments in order to effectively drown out the sounds of the Aryan Woodstock.

Down in the city of North Bay, only a couple of miles away, members of the North Bay Ministerial Association—dressed in their colorful regalia in hues of purple, crimson, green, and gold—lined the street in front of the North Bay Jewish Center. They were there to ward off any potential hostility as well as warmly greet the hundreds of worshipers of all faiths who entered the synagogue for the Saturday morning service and Bar Mitzvah celebration of Dylan Zimmer. It was a meaningful ceremony—a counter-rally of sorts, a concurrent sharing of fellowship and faith during which Reverend Frank Grey challenged the Bar Mitzvah boy to "be mindful all the rest of your life of how the spirit of God can move people to act in defiance of evil."

The confidential information Bassem had shared with me was carefully leaked to the media. It did not stop the rally but effectively took the wind out of its sails. A few weeks later, Donald Miles was found dead on the living room floor of his East Bay home, an apparent suicide. The West Coast Nazi Party was never heard from again.

But the incident spawned a warm friendship between graduate student ibn Talal and me. He even invited me to a private family party two years later when he received his master's degree in criminal justice. There he told me he would soon return to his native country, where a job was waiting for him and where he'd get married. Yet somehow I felt this would not be the last I would see of Bassem.

President Kennedy once pointed out that when written in Chinese, the word *crisis* is composed of two characters: one represents *danger*, he said, and the other represents *opportunity*.

The Aryan Woodstock incident was full of potential danger for us, but out of it came a great deal of good. It was certainly a most memorable piece of my twenty-year North Bay sojourn.

But two decades after ordination, I was good and ready for a new adventure.

CHAPTER XVIII.

AUCKLAND, NEW ZEALAND.

APRIL 1998.

If one is located outside the Land of Israel,
he should turn his face toward Israel in prayer.
If he is in the Land, he should turn toward Jerusalem.

MAIMONIDES

Unlikely as it might sound, I never experienced turning fifty. Having spoken in confidence with North Bay's board president about my intention to expand my horizons, I arranged to take some vacation time in the spring. Linda and I made ready for a trip to the Progressive Hebrew Congregation (the APHC) of Auckland, New Zealand, which, as luck would have it, was searching for a new rabbi at the very same time.

Our flight departed Honolulu on April 7 at 8:59 p.m. At nearly the exact moment the clock struck midnight to begin what should have been April 8, we crossed the International Date Line—and presto! It was April 9. So April 8 never happened for me nor for the 180 other people on that particular Air New Zealand flight. From that moment on, I felt I could rightfully claim I was forever forty-nine!

Once we settled into the motel suite the new congregation had arranged for us, we conducted our first scientific experiment in the kitchen sink. I tied a string to the old-fashioned rubber stopper and filled the sink with water. Then, pulling the stopper out carefully in an attempt to disturb the water as little as possible, we watched the water flow into the drain. I tried it once, again, and three more times. To our astonishment, it flowed clockwise. *So it's just like back home! It* doesn't *flow backward*, I thought.

Fortunately for me, James Diamond, the top local TV weatherman and a climatologist in his own right, was a member of the APHC. I had an opportunity to speak with him briefly during the visit and told him about our little experiment.

"My friends back home convinced me that the water flows backward here in the Southern Hemisphere, but my experiment proved otherwise. It all went down the drain in a clockwise direction," I told him.

Jim set me straight. "Ah yes, Rabbi," he said. "It seems every northerner makes the same mistake. Most of them—and evidently you are to be added to the list—don't bother to watch how the water flows at home before they come to New Zealand. They assume it flows clockwise in the north and therefore must flow anticlockwise, as we like to say here, Down Under. But in fact, it's just the opposite. It's in the *Northern* Hemisphere that the water flows 'backward,' or anticlockwise! It's called the Coriolis effect. Next time there's a cyclone off the Florida coast, just look at the way the clouds revolve around the eye of the storm. You'll see. We're not backward here in the Southern Hemisphere, but perhaps you fellows are!" claimed weatherman Jim with only the slightest hint of triumphalism.

During the brief visit, I thought I could detect other occasional hints of displeasure over what many Kiwis evidently feel is a kind of cultural imperialism emanating from European and American visitors.

The fact that an American had appeared as a rabbinic candidate instead of a native New Zealander was itself a bit of a cause for consternation. It stemmed from the fact that America—and to a lesser extent, England, Israel and Western Europe—are the training grounds for rabbis. The New Zealand Jewish community, scarcely seven thousand in number, is simply too small to support such a seminary. But that did not mean the Kiwis were enamored of the fact that they had to import all their rabbis.

As an American, I found New Zealand peculiar in other ways too, though I was careful not to use that term in their presence. Their sun, for example, appears to traverse the sky in the north, so people build their gardens and porches on the north side of their homes. They drive on the left side of the road, which takes quite a bit of getting used to. But even more challenging is the fact that a car's turn signal wand is found where the windshield wiper device is in American cars—that is, to the right of the steering wheel—and vice versa. The Kiwis can always tell a foreigner is behind the wheel when they see an approaching vehicle with its windshield wipers operating on a perfectly sunny day.

As progressive and enlightened as New Zealand is purported to be, some Old World biases can still be found there. Even the prime minister, Helen Clark, acknowledged in a radio interview that "New Zealand was really a very racist country" and that she was "determined to do everything [she] could as prime minister to change that." And although New Zealand can boast of more than one Jewish prime minister, a town named after one of its early

Jewish pioneers, and a number of Jewish mayors of its largest city, it can't be denied that Kiwi anti-Semitism still manifests itself in a number of ways.

I became aware of this after lunch at the posh jacket-and-tie-required One Tree Grill with attorney Clive Markson. Markson, a distinguished leader of the Jewish community, had brought me over to a nearby table and introduced me as "my friend from America" to a number of his attorney colleagues, among them some prominent movers and shakers in the city of Auckland.

As we all got up from our separate tables to leave the restaurant at about the same time, one of them asked me, "Where are you headed?"

"I'm going south to the Parnell Suites," I answered.

"Good. I live nearby," he said. "Would you like to share a taxi?"

"Certainly," I responded cheerily.

On the ride south, we chatted a bit. "Are you an attorney as well?" I asked him.

"A solicitor, yes, in private practice. In fact, my office is right across the road from the One Tree Grill."

We rode in silence for a bit, and then, out of nowhere, he told me, "Clive Markson's a Jew, you know."

"Mm-hm," was my muted response, accompanied by a half nod as we continued to converse.

It was a fact: Markson was a Jew. This gentleman, evidently, was not. Nor, he must have figured, was this American sitting next to him. But why was he telling me this—that Markson was a Jew? Did he think I was Markson's client, who should know I was dealing with a Jewish lawyer? Did this attorney sitting next to me expect me to become *his* client once I realized with whom I was dealing?

When we stopped in front of the hotel, I reached over to pay the cabbie my portion of the fare when the gentleman, perhaps having expected a more vigorous response the first time, chimed in again.

"Markson's a Jew, you know."

I opened the taxi door and scrambled out. Just before shutting the door, I looked squarely back at him and replied matter-of-factly, "I know. I'm his rabbi." I paused just long enough to glimpse the prominent citizen's pallid face turning rosy red.

The New Zealand Jewish community, I soon discovered, was a veritable United Nations. There were members from Australia, Great Britain, Canada, the United States, Israel, France, Mexico, Egypt, and Russia.

Luba Azbel, for example, was a recent Russian immigrant, a divorced mother of three, and a family physician about my age.

"Did you serve in Vietnam?" she asked me during the Oneg Shabbat social hour following my Friday night LSD trip service.

"No—thank God," I answered.

Truth was, I was in the first draft lottery in 1969. The draft people wrote all the calendar dates on 366 different table-tennis balls, threw them at random into a large bowl, and then drew out the dates one by one. If your birthday fell on the first date picked, you would be among the first to be drafted into the army. In fact, most of those born on the first one hundred drawn dates had a good chance of going to Vietnam. If your birth date was drawn toward the end of the evening, you were safe. Everyone was eligible but only for one year. My birthday came out number 312, and I was not drafted. I said to everyone I met that week, "That was the only lottery I needed to win."

"I was on the other side of that conflict," the good Russian doctor told me in her heavily accented Kiwi English. "Do you want to know what we were doing during those years?"

"Sure," I said.

"We were busy collecting bicycles from all over Russia and sending them over to North Vietnam. No doubt they were used to bring war matériel down the Ho Chi Minh Trail."

"I guess we were sort of enemies then," I joked.

"Yes. You may have lost in Vietnam, but you won the bigger war, the war against communism," she responded.

"And we're on the same side now?" I asked.

"Most definitely. We're all capitalists now."

Seeing the Vietnam War from the communist point of view was a real eye-opener for me. I was not at all a pacifist, but I certainly had not wanted to be sent into that Southeast Asian abyss.

The oddest thing for me on that visit Down Under was that it was April, with Passover just around the corner, yet the days were getting shorter and colder. Passover was supposed to be the "Festival of Spring," but there, south of the equator, it was the beginning of autumn!

As I contemplated serving the APHC, the thought of conducting the congregational Seder in the fall was quite a challenge. But fortunately there was another American rabbi in New Zealand with whom I could consult: Rabbi Matthew Isaacson, in the capital city of Wellington.

"How do you handle all the spring references in the Seder, Matthew?" I inquired in our first telephone conversation.

"It's not too hard," the senior rabbi advised. "You can explain that the ritual originated in Israel, where it *is* spring. Synagogues here across the International Date Line face Jerusalem just like synagogues everywhere around the world, so it's an object lesson. And our liturgy, as everyone knows, is peppered with references to the Promised Land. So you'll find you won't get much of an argument from the Kiwis. They admire Israel—a small, boutique country with about the same population as their own. And you could say Israel is a kind of 'island' nation too, an island of democracy in a sea of monarchies and dictatorships. And the Kiwis have come to accept, after all," he added with a laugh, "the fact that God lives in the Northern Hemisphere. They can't fight it." He couldn't resist the impulse to conclude with his favorite theological punch line.

It was true. New Zealanders hold Israel in high esteem. Israel, like New Zealand, is a can-do country where self-sufficiency is the watchword of the day.

And Israelis love New Zealand in return. Many an Israeli soldier following discharge from army service loves to come to this green, laid-back, peaceful outdoorsman's country to relax and unwind. Peaceful New Zealand has become the antidote for the hostile Middle East, the premier tourist destination for Israeli travelers—a fact not lost upon the leaders of New Zealand's tourist industry.

Toward the end of our successful tour Down Under, Linda and I decided to accept the New Zealand position. We flew home to serve out my last few months with NBJC and bid a tearful farewell to our two grown children, along with relatives and friends.

We would somehow find a way to pay for young David's tuition at the U of M, but to do so would necessitate considerable downsizing for us. So we put our modest North Bay home on the market and found a delightful two-bedroom apartment in Devonport, an attractive village-like suburb across the bay from downtown Auckland. We planned to commute by ferry most days. But for the inevitable late-night meetings that would end after the last ferry's departure, we would have to take the congregation car—which meant we'd have to get used to driving on the left side of the road.

It would be a small price to pay for what promised to be another great adventure. But first, I would need to bring our North Bay sojourn to its conclusion.

CHAPTER XIX.

 NORTH BAY. NOVEMBER 1998.

Every new beginning comes from some other beginning's end.

Seneca

I accepted the New Zealand position but with some mixed feelings. It was clearly time to leave, but it wouldn't be easy. In my
farewell address to the NBJC, I drew upon an earlier leave-taking
and spoke about my kibbutz friend Uriel Dagan.

> As you all know, before I became a rabbi I spent
> a fair bit of time driving a tractor on a kibbutz in
> Israel. There I met a man named Uriel, the kibbutz
> scholar. Every kibbutz seems to have such a scholar,
> and usually only one. Someone who has studied the
> history of the Land—its geography, its archaeology,
> its flora and fauna—and can impart this knowledge
> in an effective way to the kibbutz public.
>   Uriel was the scholar of Kibbutz Haziv. He was
> a fabulous teacher. He knew every rock, every hill,
> and every valley of the Land of Israel and could tell
> the story of each place in a most exceptional way.

He had the uncanny ability to make the Bible's narratives virtually leap out of the pages wherever we would go. Over the past few decades, I have traveled the length and breadth of the Holy Land with you, and we have heard many guides tell their stories. But Uriel could make that land come alive as no one else could.

Born in Jerusalem and educated at the Hebrew University, he could have easily become a professor of biblical studies or Jewish history in Jerusalem or Los Angeles or New York or Oxford. But he married a daughter of the kibbutz and chose to remain there, where, in addition to conducting the occasional field trip for kibbutz members and guests, he taught in the regional high school.

But to my displeasure, the men of the kibbutz would almost never miss an opportunity to disparage my friend Uriel at our men's afternoon tea gatherings. "Uriel, yeah," one or another would scoff, "he knows his Bible, but he's all thumbs." Or "Uriel, ha!" another would chime in. "He's a good teacher, but all he has are two left hands." Time and again when Uriel's name would come up, my fellow workers would snicker at his expense, and then we would go on to another topic.

On a kibbutz, as we all know, the ability to work well and creatively with one's hands is the most coveted skill; that's what was valued there. And by that standard, Uriel was not a very able worker. His contribution was not at all well regarded. So he was derided for what he *couldn't* do rather than lauded for what he *could* do.

"But he's such a great scholar," I would argue in his defense. "Isn't that important too?" I was not afraid to speak up and plead Uriel's case in my company of men, but my pleas always fell on deaf ears.

One day, out of frustration, I approached Uriel. I asked him why he chose to stay on that kibbutz—where he knew he was scoffed at for what seemed to be his one deficiency—when he could have just as well gone somewhere else and become an esteemed professor of Judaic studies in Tel Aviv or London or Boston. His answer was most enlightening, flavored with characteristic Jewish modesty and humility.

"For me it is no problem," he told me. "You see, Yonatan, I can only *teach* history, but these kibbutzniks here are *making* history. And because I cannot do what they *can* do, here, on this kibbutz, I feel more complete. Here I am fulfilled."

When my son, David, was about five years old, a somewhat similar conversation took place. We were walking one day to a nearby park when he saw some parents lift their son from his wheelchair into their car at the end of their visit to the park.

As we passed by, David said to me that he wished he were disabled.

"Why would you say that?" I asked him in horror.

He responded with all the innocence of a five-year-old: "Because disabled kids get hugged more."

With that, of course, I picked him up and hugged him and carried him a distance. I realized then that through his very young and sensitive eyes, being disabled *did* have its benefits. Even at his tender age, David could see an advantage in being disadvantaged; he could perceive something favorable in what was to all other outward appearances an unfavorable circumstance.

Neither Uriel, the kibbutz scholar, nor my son, David, might have known it at the time, but they were both echoing to me the teaching of a famous Hasidic master, Menaḥem Mendl of Kotzk, the Kotzker Rebbe. He famously said, "We can become more complete when we have something missing. We can become more whole when we are broken. And there is nothing so whole as a broken heart," a paradoxical teaching that nevertheless makes a great deal of sense. The great rabbi was teaching that we all are broken in one way or another.

Where would the Kotzker Rebbe learn such a teaching? I'm certain he learned it from the Hebrew Bible, where we discover that virtually *all* of our ancestors had major deficiencies.

Abraham, for example—the great Abraham is in reality a broken father, unable to communicate with his son Isaac, and unable to assert himself even in his own household. Isaac is introverted almost to a fault, and when he becomes a father, he seems to care for nothing more than his own appetite. Rachel is portrayed as a thief and a liar.

Rebecca is a conniver and a manipulator. Moses—even Moses, who is called upon to articulate the most compelling summons in all of human history—even Moses suffers, like England's George VI, from an inability to speak well.

But the most broken of all our biblical heroes is Jacob, whose name means, "the heel"; Jacob, who bamboozles his brother and tricks his father and acts like a heel throughout his early life. Young Jacob is the most broken of all.

But it is here that our Torah teaches us a most important lesson. Here the tradition conveys an essential Jewish teaching, the lesson that human beings are not created as a finished product, a "once and for all," as it were. The point of our biblical heroes' biographies is that each of them evolves. They all get better as they get older; they mature morally and spiritually as they go through life. And what is fascinating, in light of the Kotzker Rebbe's teaching, is that it begins to happen *after* they are wounded in some way.

It begins to happen to Jacob, for example, only after he has sustained a physical handicap! Only after Jacob is injured in his encounter with the angel does his character begin to change. He is stricken, and he suddenly begins to soften. A man who once spent his days and nights scheming to outwit someone or another, Jacob becomes a true *mentsch*. And then—and only then—does he acquire the name Israel, after whom we are all named. And it is only after he has been hobbled by his injury that the

Bible says of Jacob, *"vayavo Yaakov shalem"*—"Jacob became whole."

I've never seen the Golestan Palace in Tehran, but I understand that when you walk into the entry foyer, you are greeted by a dazzling display of light.

Originally, as the story goes, when the palace was designed, the architect specified huge glass mirrors to be placed on the walls. But when the first shipment of mirrors arrived from Paris, the workmen found to their horror that the mirrors had been shattered in transit.

The contractor threw them into the trash and brought the sad news to the architect.

But amazingly, the architect ordered all the broken shards to be collected from the trash bins, and when they were gathered before him, he did an astonishing thing. He smashed them into tiny pieces and ordered the workmen to glue the tiny pieces onto the walls and columns to become a mosaic of silvery, shimmering bits of glass. As you walk through that grand entrance today, I am told, you begin to think that the domed ceiling, the side walls, and the columns are covered with diamonds until you discover that the rainbow of colors is produced by small pieces of glass reflecting the light.

They were shattered, then pieced together, only to become more beautiful. They were broken, only to become more whole.

And isn't it a fact of life that when one of our senses is missing, the remaining ones become more acute, as if to compensate for the loss? Isn't it true that blind people often develop more sensitive hearing, for example? That those who are consigned to wheelchairs often develop tremendous upper body strength? And isn't it a fact that when we are missing a part of our selves, other parts become stronger to make up for the loss? As the Kotzker Rebbe taught so perceptively, we can become more whole when we are broken.

The men of the Kibbutz Haziv would snicker whenever my friend Uriel's name came up, until the day when one of them ended the conversation once and for all.

"Kol ehad im ha hesronot shelo," he said emphatically. Or, "Everyone is deficient in some way."

And I breathed a sigh of relief. Finally, this kibbutz colleague was saying that Uriel was like all the rest of us, implying that it is a good thing, a healthy thing, for each of us to be confronted with our own inadequacies. It was a bit of Jewish folk wisdom that can be traced all the way back to the Kotzker Rebbe.

I chose to share this sermon with you now because my own heart is somewhat broken tonight as I bid farewell to you after twenty years of service. But it's clearly time for me to move on, and for you as well. Despite the loss that I feel, I am looking forward to a new chapter in my life in which I hope to develop new skills and new abilities to help me through the challenges that lie ahead. And I know this congregation will be strengthened too as it looks for a new leader to take the rabbinical reins.

William Shakespeare was really on to something when he said, "Parting is such sweet sorrow." I know that sweet sorrow now. And I believe the Kotzker Rebbe shared a similar sentiment when he taught, "There is nothing so whole as a broken heart."

Many have been the joys and triumphs of these past two decades while I have had the privilege of serving this wonderful community. I will cherish the memories forever.

Shabbat shalom and *L'hitraot. Au revoir,* my good friends.

PART III
DOWN UNDER

CHAPTER XX.

 AUCKLAND. FINAL DAYS OF

THE TWENTIETH CENTURY.

I have spread you abroad like the four winds of the sky.

ZEḤARIA 2:10

Linda and I quickly discovered that there are only two types of Judaism Down Under—"Orthodox" and "Progressive"—in contrast to the wide variety of movements and streams in North America. We learned that non-Orthodox Judaism outside North America falls under the umbrella of the World Union for Progressive Judaism. That's why it's officially called "Progressive" rather than "Reform," which is the more common term in North America.

What's the difference between Orthodox and Progressive Judaism? Orthodox Jews believe that the Hebrew Bible was communicated directly by God to Moses, and through Moses, to the entire Jewish people. They believe in the literal truth of the Bible, that the revelation of that truth happened exactly as it is recounted chiefly in the Book of Exodus and, to a lesser degree, in the other thirty-eight books of the Hebrew Bible.

Reform or Progressive Jews, on the other hand, believe that God-inspired human beings, rather than a single Divine Being, composed the Bible out of their own life experiences over many centuries.

Orthodox Jews believe that Jewish Law, written by the great rabbis some centuries after the Bible was canonized, regulates Jewish daily life down to the minutest detail with the same force of authority—and according to some rabbis, an even greater degree of authority—than the Hebrew Bible upon which it is based.

Progressive Jews believe these laws are customs or folkways, and though widely practiced, they do not carry the same weight of authority. Progressive Jews hold that the customs and traditions that help define us as Jews can nevertheless be modified as the life process of the Jewish people carries us into new areas of the world and new eras of history.

My calling Heather Tuchman up to the Torah was an example of just such a modification. Bringing instrumental music into the Sabbath service is another. Driving one's automobile on the Sabbath was yet another practice introduced to enable Progressive Jews to live anywhere within driving—as opposed to walking—distance from their synagogue. We Progressive Jews like to say, "Tradition has a vote, but not a veto."

The first Jewish settlers in New Zealand were Englishmen who arrived early in the nineteenth century, shortly after Captain James Cook explored the islands. Because the reform of Judaism had not yet taken hold, they knew only orthodoxy. But they were compelled by their new circumstances, nevertheless, to modify their religious practices.

For instance, unlike other Jewish pioneers who "imported" their Jewish brides from England and elsewhere once they settled in the New World, some Jewish pioneers in New Zealand married local Maori women even in the absence of the bride's conversion to Judaism. Some of their descendants practice Judaism to this day, but one can also find Maori men and women of various religious denominations with surnames such as Abrahams, Daniels, Levi, Levin, Nathan, and Samuels—surnames inherited from their Jewish ancestors.

Eventually, the Jewish pioneers established synagogues in the more populous New Zealand cities of Auckland, Wellington, and Christchurch. The largest synagogue in the country is Auckland's Orthodox synagogue, located near the Central Business District.

Upon entering the impressive building for the first time, Linda and I viewed New Zealand's first Hebrew marriage contract, written in 1841, proudly on display in the foyer along with other documents chronicling New Zealand Jewish history. Evidently, the Jewish-born bride in this case had been previously married to a ship's captain who died at sea. As there were no Hebrew scribes in the new country at the time, the immigrant bride brought her original marriage contract, her ketubah, to the new marriage so it could be copied and altered in the appropriate places. Only one man in the entire country was well versed enough in the sacred tongue to attempt to make the appropriate changes.

But when I read the document, I burst out laughing.

"What's so funny, JJ?" Linda asked.

"Well," I explained, "the scribe who copied this ketubah did a pretty good job. He was a layman, after all. But on this line," I continued, pointing to the document now encased in glass, "he forgot to change the term for the bride's status at the time of this, her second marriage. In her first marriage contract, of course, she was identified as a *betulah*, a virgin. But the New Zealand scribe forgot—or else did not know—to change the term to *almanah*, a widow, for her second marriage. So, this ketubah indicates that although she was married to her first husband for a number of years, she was still a virgin at the time of her second marriage! How likely is that?"

I couldn't contain my amusement, especially because no one else was around.

"Well, it's possible," said Linda with a twinkle in her eye. "After all, a ship's captain spends a great deal of time at sea."

We arrived in New Zealand in November. That meant our first High Holy Days Down Under wouldn't be celebrated until the following September. And what an auspicious beginning to the Jewish New Year it turned out to be! President Bill Clinton had come to town for the Asia-Pacific Economic Cooperation (APEC) conference, which was scheduled to begin on Rosh Hashanah. Dorothy Rodham, his mother-in-law, accompanied him—a fact that caused one Auckland gossip columnist to murmur, "Well, somebody's got to chaperone that bloke."

We didn't think we'd see the president in the synagogue, but we knew some of his top aides would be there. We were amused to see how our neighboring Orthodox synagogue tried to attract delegates to their Rosh Hashanah service, putting out the word that they were "Orthodox light" or, better yet, Conservative. But we were pretty confident that no matter how our Orthodox neighbors might portray themselves, neither United States Trade Representative Charlene Barshefsky nor Special Advisor to the President

Wendy Sherman would allow themselves to be seated in a separate women's section if a Progressive alternative could be found. And we were right.

Secret Service people arrived at the APHC the day before the holiday, sweeping the entire building and grounds with their electronic devices and their dogs. We strategized with the Secret Service to decide where the various dignitaries would be seated and pinned "seat taken" notices to those spots. We also reserved special places for their "minders," a common Down Under term for bodyguards. We were informed that the minders would be armed, however inconspicuously.

About twenty minutes before the morning service was to begin, two large black limousines pulled up to the synagogue as four people alighted from each. We stood outside to greet Barshefsky and Sherman along with members of their entourages. We escorted them inside. We were surprised to discover that the drivers remained at the ready as both limousines kept their engines running throughout the two-hour-long service, a necessary security measure. But with gas at more than five dollars per gallon, the American delegates' Rosh Hashanah experience would cost a pretty penny for the American taxpayer, despite the Clinton administration's $4 billion budget surplus.

Another big surprise was the delegates' Hebrew proficiency. I happened to glance over, for example, at Ms. Barshefsky during the reading of the selection from the First Book of Samuel. There was Ms. Barshefsky sitting in the front row, mouthing each word in Hebrew along with the reader and chanting quietly along with him. All the delegates and their minders, I'm pleased to report, participated wholeheartedly throughout the service, one of the longest of the year. When it was over, they mingled briefly with our members, then were whisked off in their awaiting limousines for an important luncheon with the president.

It turned out well that the APEC conference was scheduled in mid-September that year. Had it taken place a couple of months later, hotel rooms would have been hard to find. As the year 1999 drew to a close, faraway New Zealand would become the center of the world, first to greet the dawn of the new millennium.

CHAPTER XXI.

✈ AUCKLAND. DAWN OF THE NEW MILLENNIUM.

In the end, you will all belong to me.

Folk Parable

The advent of the new millennium brought a great deal of attention to the small island nation of New Zealand. A bright international spotlight would soon focus on the tiny boutique country, highlighting both its considerable assets as well as its liabilities.

The world now learned that New Zealand, while part of the British Commonwealth with a large Caucasian majority, is also home to a profusion of Polynesian communities from throughout the South Pacific. Chief among them are the native New Zealand Maori. Roughly 18 percent of New Zealand's population identifies as Maori or of Maori descent.

One well-known Maori citizen, Tipene Solomon, was baptized in the Catholic Church but converted to Judaism as a young adult and became an active member of the Auckland Progressive Hebrew Congregation.

Tipene—whose chosen Hebrew name is Shimshon, meaning, appropriately, Samson—cuts quite a figure in the city of Auckland. He stands a full six feet four inches tall and weighs a hefty 297 pounds—as formidable as any American NFL lineman. He has fierce, dark Maori features but does his best to soften his intimidating appearance with a soothing voice and an easy smile.

Not surprisingly, Tipene played rugby in high school but found he did not possess the ruthlessness or enough of the killer instinct to make a career of it. Instead, he became a social worker in the employ of the New Zealand national social services department. But because of New Zealand's unique location just west of the International Date Line, social worker Tipene Solomon would soon become an international television star.

It all began to happen a few days before the dawn of the new millennium, when legions of documentary filmmakers and international television news crews descended upon New Zealand to film the first sunrise of the year 2000. Among the many filmmakers and journalists was a crew from Israel's Channel 2 television.

Along with their intention to film the first dawn, Channel 2 came to town to explore what was then thought to be a unique relationship between New Zealand's indigenous Maori people and the Jews. At the time, a rumor circulated in Israel about a Maori group claiming to be descendants of one of the Ten Lost Tribes. Tipene, who was also known as Steve, was pointed out to them as someone who could shed some light on the subject.

Armed with monstrous cameras and sound equipment, the journalists set up their ad hoc studio in the APHC sanctuary—a modern room filled with natural sunlight and furnished with warm wooden pews, burgundy carpets, and blue mosaic-tile accents throughout. As the cameras began to roll, Tipene, in traditional Maori fashion, introduced himself by first indicating his tribe.

"I am Tipene, or Shimshon, Solomon," he said. "My *iwi*, or tribe, is the Ngāti Tauranga." He then went on to identify his mountain and the principal river that runs through his tribal land.

The television interviewer next asked him if he were Jewish.

"My Jewish ancestor was Samuel Solomon, who married the young Maori woman Manama Henare. They were my father's great-grandparents. I was baptized in the Catholic Church but became fully Jewish when I converted at the age of twenty-two."

Then came the pivotal question: "Are the Maori people one of the Ten Lost Tribes of Israel?"

"I don't actually believe so," he replied. "I think what happened is this: When the English missionaries began to convert my people, they told them stories of both the Hebrew Bible *and* the Christian Bible, the Old and the New Testaments. My forebears *loved* the Old Testament narratives—stories about the tribal allotment of land, about conflicts between the tribes, about the wars of the Israelites, about celebrating the topography and living off the fruit of the land. My Maori ancestors would listen to these stories with rapt attention. They could certainly identify with them, a thousand times more readily than with New Testament stories about *love* and *forgiveness* and *turning the other cheek*."

He related the last few words in a somewhat disdainful tone. After all, he came from noble warrior stock.

Then he went on. "So I think my ancestors were ready to accept the new religion once they were assured it contained the Old Testament along with the New Testament. But I don't believe there is a biological connection between the ancient Hebrews and the Maori."

As he came to the end of his impressive chronicle, a sly grin broke out across his face.

"I'm certain there is no biological connection, in fact—how could there be?" he asked, leaning forward now and peering directly into the camera, getting ready to deliver his knockout punch. "My Maori ancestors knew how to navigate with pinpoint accuracy across vast, immeasurable oceans with little to guide them other than ocean currents and the heavenly stars—while my Jewish ancestors got lost in the desert for forty long years!"

They say all of Israel broke out in laughter when Channel 2 broadcast that interview. They laughed, then breathed a sigh of relief. *Whew!* Israel had enough problems with housing and unemployment as it was. The Maori would not claim to be yet another "Lost Tribe" and demand automatic Israeli citizenship with all its appended benefits under the Law of Return.

Thank heavens for that!

Tipene was an articulate spokesman for the Maori culture and could move gracefully through a number of ethnic subcultures. He often pointed out to me that New Zealand's Maori population was roughly the same percentage as Israel's Arab population. He was proud of the fact that his native New Zealand is one of perhaps only a handful of countries that have navigated the binational dilemma successfully, and he suggested the New Zealand experiment could serve as a model for other binational countries.

When the British settled in the country in the early nineteenth century, they drew up a treaty with the native Maori population, guaranteeing certain rights and territories to the Maori in perpetuity. At the same time, the treaty granted both groups the rights and privileges of citizens of the British Empire. The agreement is called the Treaty of Waitangi, the signing of which is celebrated as a national holiday, Waitangi Day, each February.

At its founding, New Zealand granted minority rights that Australia and America, for example, have taken more than two centuries to achieve. It's encouraging, however, to observe that progress toward reconciliation has been made on both the American and Australian continents.

Of course, many issues remain in all three countries. In New Zealand, one still hears opposing points of view nearly two centuries after the nation's founding. The English text of the Treaty of Waitangi, for example, differs in some respects from the Maori translation. And to this day one can find Maori people who claim to be the rightful "owners" of the land. However begrudgingly—and after a number of nineteenth-century battles known as the Land Wars—they now accept the presence of European "guests."

Even I unexpectedly found myself immersed in this debate while on the Devonport ferry after a late night at the synagogue. It was a delightful evening illuminated brightly by a full moon. I was alone on the back deck, breathing in the fresh evening air, when out of the main cabin came a young, slightly inebriated Maori gentleman.

"This is *my* land," the Maori man claimed in a loud voice to no one in particular as he tramped back and forth along the rear deck, waving his right hand over the harbor. "This is all Maori land. We were here first."

I tried to ignore the outburst, but then he came closer and pointed directly at me.

"You're on *my* land. This is *my* land," he added in a mildly threatening way.

As his harangue now included me, I couldn't hold back. I nodded a couple of times to indicate I understood his point of view. And then, in a flash of inspiration, I pointed up at the full moon.

"Do you see that—the moon up there?" I asked the Maori gentleman.

He was now swaying back and forth, an obvious effect of both the harbor waves and his state of insobriety.

"Yeah," he replied.

"That's *my* land." I paused to let the words sink in. "That's *my* land up there. I'm an American. We were *there* first."

A stunned silence followed my words as the puzzled New Zealander tried to comprehend what I was saying. He shook his head, looked up at the moon, then looked back at me. With a confused half smile and another shake of his head, he blurted out a long, emphatic "*Naaaaah!*" and went back inside the main cabin.

So, who *does* own the land? The Maori descend from Polynesian warriors who, according to their own oral history, originated in an area of the Pacific Ocean that is today called the Cook Islands. When they came upon New Zealand, they named it Aotearoa, "the Land of the Long White Cloud." They may have found Aotearoa empty of human inhabitants. But when they landed in the nearby Chatham Islands, they found an indigenous group, the Moriori, already in residence. Maori history then goes on to relate unabashedly how the new settlers all but wiped out the indigenous population: they killed them, then they ate them. It is not a pretty story.

Who owns the land? The ones who get there first? Or the ones with the more powerful army? How did we Americans come to "own" Texas, for example, after all?

I got a fascinating personal perspective on this very subject one day at a preview screening of the 2005 film *Munich*, arranged by the movie editor of the *New Zealand Post*. I was seated next to an Israeli Arab and asked him, "Where are you from in the Holy Land?"

"A Christian village in the north called Kafr Yasif, near the city of Akko," he answered back. "We have a large Muslim minority and some Druze as well. The Roman general Josephus mentioned my village in his first-century book."

I chose not to argue with the man, who was affable enough, about his account. He may have been historically correct to a degree: Josephus did, in fact, become a citizen of Rome. But his birth name was Yosef ben Matityahu; he was a Jewish general in the rebellion against Rome in 67 CE. He later traded sides and wrote a history of the war. And when he named Kafr Yasif in his book, he counted it as one of thirty-five Jewish villages in that region of the Galilee.

So what happened to the Jews of Kafr Yasif? Did they abandon their village or abandon their faith? Some historians claim that many Palestinians are actually descended from Jews who managed to avoid being deported over the past two thousand years or who returned to the land after they were exiled. One thing many Palestinian Jews were unable to avoid, however, was conversion to Christianity or Islam. Historians point, as one example among many, to the Muslim owners of the famous Abulafia bakery of Jaffa, who acknowledge that they are direct descendants of the legendary Rabbi Abraham Abulafia.

The fact that Kafr Yasif is today identified as an Israeli Arab village is an illustration of the dilemma posed by the question, "Who owns the land?" It points to the fact that much of Israel's

Jewish history—including the names of its villages and towns—has been absorbed by Israeli Arabs and incorporated into their own narrative. An obscure irony of the whole situation is that we and they are, by and large, descendants of the very same ancestors, now verified by DNA research!

I once heard a story about the leaders of two contending peoples arguing over this very question of ownership of the land: The leader of the first group contends that the land belongs to *his* people, while the other leader makes the same claim.

Finally, an observer chimes in and says, "Because you two obviously cannot agree, let's listen to what the land has to say."

So they kneel down and put their ears to the ground. They then hear the land whisper up back to them, "In the end, you will *all* belong to *me*."

CHAPTER XXII.

 AUCKLAND. FEBRUARY 2006.

Rabbi Yoḥanan asked his disciples, "What is the best quality for a person to acquire?" Rabbi Shimon answered, "The ability to foresee the consequences of his actions."

PIRKEI AVOT: SAYINGS OF THE FATHERS, CHAPTER II

"Why don't you and Linda apply for your Kiwi passports?" Matthew Isaacson, my Wellington colleague, suggested one day. "After all, one can never be too rich, too thin, or have too many passports. You've already lived here more than the required five years, so the path to citizenship should be clear."

Matthew and his wife, Ruth, had become New Zealand citizens, so why not Linda and I? And as long as we didn't volunteer for the New Zealand Army, we could remain American citizens as well. It would all be kosher and aboveboard. So in 2004, we were sworn in as Kiwi citizens and shortly thereafter received our highly prized New Zealand passports.

We were well aware that a New Zealand passport is among the most coveted passports in the entire world. Because New Zealand strives to have friendly relations with every other nation, its citizens are welcomed with open arms throughout the globe. And New Zealand, in turn, has opened *its* arms to refugees seeking a safe haven from scenes of conflict throughout the globe. I have seen joy on the faces of such refugees when they acquire citizenship along with all the associated benefits and privileges, including the right to obtain a New Zealand passport.

New Zealand has always appealed, in particular, to Europeans looking for an escape. It's about as far away from Europe as a person can travel—halfway around the world longitudinally, west to east, as well as latitudinally, north to south. As a result of the island nation's geographic remoteness, many Europeans fleeing their past have made their tortuous way to faraway New Zealand to acquire new identities and begin afresh. This was true of Jews attempting to escape Nazi Germany and also true of Nazis trying to escape postwar Germany.

This fact was brought home one evening as I sat in my office with a man named Erik Martin from the nearby city of Hamilton. He had called our temple secretary, Nadine, to set an evening appointment so he could finish his workday at the Huntly Power Station, where he was employed as a hydraulic systems engineer. He asked Nadine for directions, so we were fairly certain he had never before set foot in the building.

Erik was then in his late fifties, with light-brown hair, dark eyes, and pale skin. He stood about five foot six. When I assured him we were the only two to be found in the building, he took a slightly yellowed sheet of card stock out of his briefcase.

It was divided into two sections with a vertical line down the middle. At the very top was the German word *Personalausweis*— identity card—accompanied by a fading blue WWII Third Reich eagle stamp. His name was written in black ink on a line at the bottom along with his birthday, 21 March 1941.

On the left side above his name was a black-and-white photograph of a Luftwaffe pilot resplendent in his Nazi uniform with officer's cap. As the typewritten name indicated, it was Martin's father. Above the photo were the names and birth dates of his father's parents.

There were three names on the left side of the sheet. The right side was an entirely different story. Toward the bottom, opposite Erik's father, appeared a photo of his mother, née Anna Weiss—a pleasant-looking dark-haired, dark-eyed woman born in 1906. Above her were the names of her parents; above them, her grandparents; and above them, squeezed together on the very top line, were the eight names and birth dates of her great-grandparents. I noticed the birth date of one of her great-grandfathers: 1796!

The sheet was perfectly clear, but I had never seen anything like it before. I had heard rumors, of course, about intermarried German Jews who survived the war. But never in my wildest imagination did I believe a Jewish woman could be married to a Luftwaffe captain and live long enough to have a child by him in the middle of the war.

Unable to control my astonishment, I blurted out: "Your mother is Jewish!"

"Yes," Erik acknowledged. He seemed pleased to observe my incredulity. "She told me that as long as my father was alive, we were safe during the war, even though we were somewhat socially ostracized. But when my father was shot down over Abbeville, France, in 1943, my mother said we became very vulnerable. We escaped to Spain and stayed there with members of her family who had arrived earlier. Then she brought me to New Zealand right after the war."

"This is quite amazing, Erik. What is it that I can help you with?" I had calmed down a little by then.

"Well, Rabbi, I want to know if this document says that I am Jewish."

"Without a doubt, Erik. In fact, very few people around here can produce documentation like this to prove their Jewish identity." It was ironic but true. "Even the most Orthodox among us hold that Jewish identity is passed through the mother. This shows that not only was your mother Jewish, but her mother, her grandmothers, and her great-grandmothers as well. Is your mother still living?"

"She died five years ago," he replied. "My mother asked to be cremated—'to be with my family who never made it out,' she said. Yet she so loved the ocean that she asked me to scatter her ashes off Great Barrier Island. But I came to talk with you about my own future. I'm not married, and I have no children. I wanted to know if I can be buried in the Jewish cemetery at Waikumete."

As Erik apparently knew, Waikumete Cemetery, located in a suburb of Auckland, was New Zealand's largest public burial ground. It included a number of sections devoted to various ethnic and religious groups, among them a Progressive Jewish section, an Orthodox Jewish section, and a historic Jewish section dating from the early nineteenth century. He may not have known, however, that we were then in the process of establishing a fourth "shared community section" for intermarried couples who chose to be buried together.

"Yes, I'm sure it can be arranged," I answered him truthfully. "But you're still young. Why don't you consider becoming part of our community? We have a few members in Hamilton who attend our Sunday morning religious school, which also has an adult education component. Do you know the Robinsons down there? They come up just about every weekend."

He didn't respond to my suggestion. Instead, he said, rather seriously, "Do you have a copy machine here, Rabbi? I'd like you to keep a copy of this identity card in your office."

"Certainly. Just one minute," I replied, then went into the secretary's office and made two copies of the extraordinary document.

As he headed out the front door—Erik Martin, son of a Jewish mother and a World War II Luftwaffe officer—turned to me and said, "Rabbi, I have terminal cancer. I'd like to be buried in the Jewish cemetery. Please see that it is done."

And then in a quiet display of European courtesy, he gave a little bow and said, "I thank you." His voice was remarkably restrained given the news he was now conveying to me.

After a brief moment to catch my breath, I told him, "Yes, of course, Erik. Of course."

Three days later, I was getting ready to head home to Devonport when I heard a loud rumbling noise outside the temple. It was Sunday afternoon. The Community Guardian Group (CGG), an organization of young adults whose mission was to safeguard local Jewish institutions and events, was expected for its weekly training session at any minute. I was well aware that the CGG preferred to train in secrecy, but I was staying late after Sunday school to hurry through some paperwork. As eager as I might have been to observe the training session, I knew I should try to get out of their way.

But if the thundering sound of a half dozen motorcycles coming down Newmarket Road had anything to do with the training session, then it was not going to be a very clandestine meeting. And it was going to begin earlier than anticipated.

As I peered out my window, I saw them: six olive-skinned, dark-haired men casually dressed, all rather average in height. They pulled their motorcycles up over the curb and parked them on the temple's front lawn, where a low stone fence and a row of bushes would shield them from the street. What was noticeable about them is that they were not especially noticeable, neither as individuals nor as a group.

But leading them down the walkway was someone I recognized quite readily, on the other hand. Someone reasonably taller than the others and with fairer skin. It was a figure I hadn't seen in thirty years, but he was still easy to identify, still physically fit, and only very slightly stooped.

The visitor tried to open the door with his own set of keys. Upon hearing him struggle with the lock for some time, I decided to open it for him from the inside.

"*Shalom*, Benjamin Braham. Welcome to the APHC," I greeted him in a friendly tone of voice.

With his left index finger held tightly against his pursed lips, the visitor held out his right hand for me to shake. Then he said with a wink, "I go by Ben Skooler these days, Jonatha—ah, Rabbi." Then, looking about to see if anyone else was around, he continued, "I didn't expect to see you still here this late in the afternoon. How have you been?"

It was clear Banjo was not at all surprised to find me in Auckland.

"You know I am the new Community Guardian Group director, do you not?" he asked.

"No, as a matter of fact, I hadn't heard that. I mean, I didn't know it was you," I replied matter-of-factly. "Are you here for the training?"

"Yes, that's right. But first, I wanted to show the building to some friends—that's why we've come a bit early," Banjo said. He hadn't lost his Aussie accent even though he had lived in Israel for over half a century.

"And who are these people?" I asked.

Coming toward us now down the walkway were the six men, doffing their motorcycle helmets as they approached, all apparently in their late twenties and early thirties. They did not look like Aucklanders, and they spoke Hebrew with a peculiar accent. Not quite Arabic, not quite Russian—an accent that came, perhaps, from somewhere in the region where north and south Asia meet.

I guessed they might be Iranian Jews. In North Bay, I had come across a number of Persian Jews who had fled from Iran when the shah was deposed. This group of men looked and sounded somewhat like them. By now, the first decade of the twenty-first century, Jewish children born in the latter years of the deposed shah's regime would have, indeed, reached their twenties and thirties.

"These people," answered Banjo, pausing for a moment while greeting each one as they entered, "*this* is my *family*."

I suddenly remembered how Banjo would disappear from the kibbutz for days on end, apparently on secret government business. I also knew that the director of the Community Guardian Group was usually a Mossad man on leave. So, putting two and two together, I came to the conclusion that by "family," Banjo meant something like "my band of brothers." It all began to make sense.

"Okay, Ben, uh, Skooler. Have a good time. I see you have your own set of keys, so don't forget to lock the door behind you."

"Ken, ken, Yonatan. Al tidag," Banjo replied. Or, "Yes, Yes, Jonathan. Don't worry."

He had entered New Zealand as Ben Skooler on a false South African passport, ostensibly as a private tourist with a self-chosen volunteer mission: to conduct three months of training for the CGG.

But in a few weeks, the real purpose behind the sudden appearance of Benjamin Braham and his "family" would become obvious to everyone—and known throughout the world.

CHAPTER XXIII.

 AUCKLAND. MARCH 2006.

Secrecy is the first essential in affairs of state.

CARDINAL RICHELIEU

I would see Benjamin Braham only one more time during his Auckland sojourn. He was standing on a low wall surveying the crowd gathering on Aotea Square for the annual Purim celebration. I snapped a few photos of "Ben Skooler" with his walkie-talkie in hand, but as I came closer, he waved me off to indicate, "No. No photos."

As I had suspected during our earlier chance encounter, Banjo had every reason to be secretive about his presence in Auckland. I guessed he was by now a senior officer in Israel's intelligence service, operating under cover for some purpose I did not, as yet, comprehend.

What I did understand was that Israel's Institute for Intelligence and Special Operations—or Mossad, as it is more popularly known—faces challenges other intelligence services do not face. When the CIA or the British MI6 sends an operative into the field, they can usually provide him or her with a valid American or British passport issued in the name of a false identity. But an Israeli operative cannot use an Israeli passport; most of the countries in which he or she will be acting do not have diplomatic relations with Israel.

For this reason, the need to obtain foreign passports—by any means necessary—is an acute one. In particular, Mossad tries to acquire passports from neutral countries with access to the greatest number of possible ports of entry.

At the time, New Zealand passports were especially welcomed in the Arab world—not only because of the country's vaunted neutrality but also because of its flocks. New Zealand, famous for the fact that it produced eighteen sheep for every citizen, was in the enviable position of chief purveyor of live sheep to the Arab world. Prime Minister Helen Clark pushed hard to raise New Zealand's profile in the Middle East and increase lamb production at home. Wealthy Arab customers in oil-rich nations began to take note, especially after a sheep-disease scandal in Australia gave the Kiwis a leg up on the competition, so to speak. Along with their farm products, New Zealand residents, inveterate travelers all, continued to be welcomed with open arms throughout the Middle East.

I now have no doubt this was the primary purpose behind Benjamin Braham's New Zealand visit: a brazen scheme to procure some of the world's most highly prized passports.

His method was apparently quite simple. He assigned an eighth member of his team, an Australian, to secure temporary employment with Parassist Auckland, an institution for adults with severe physical disabilities. In this position, the Australian could easily access files of men around the age of Banjo's team members. The team would set up telephone service and a fake post office box in the name of one of their identity-theft victims from Parassist, then they'd quickly send in a passport application. Before the authorities could connect the dots, Banjo's team member would be out of the country with his new passport carefully tucked away.

Three passports were procured this way. Banjo's scheme was bold, simple in concept, audacious in plan—but as it would soon become apparent, it was remarkably sloppy in its execution. Under the guise of Ben Skooler, Banjo was now in his late sixties and evidently starting to lose his edge.

With the fourth passport application, a passport officer made a routine follow-up telephone inquiry. He discovered the "applicant" on the other end of the line had a distinct foreign accent. His suspicion now aroused, the officer phoned the father of the man named on the application and discovered that the application was a fraud. A sting operation was quickly put in place.

I have no proof that Banjo Braham was involved. I have no proof—and at the same time no doubt. The fact that the very next Community Guardian Group training session was abruptly canceled was evidence enough for me.

With his scheme quickly unraveling, Banjo and his Kibbutz Haziv wife, Yael, must have hurriedly packed their suitcases and flown out of the country, managing to escape only by the skin of their teeth. He was never connected with the crime, but I was certain he had been the one pulling the strings.

Within hours of Banjo's departure, Auckland police descended on two of his "family" members caught in the passport fraud scheme set up by their puppet master. The arrest, trial, and imprisonment of the Israeli spies made headlines around the world.

Foolhardy Israel, I thought to myself when I heard the news, *trying to pull the wool over the eyes of the planet's foremost dealers in wool!*

In all likelihood, Mossad approached the New Zealand Security Intelligence Service, the NZSIS, in an attempt to get the incident handled quietly. But according to the report I read, Prime Minister Clark would not play along, insisting the men be brought to trial as well as dismissing Israel's New Zealand ambassador. In a later WikiLeaks revelation, the American ambassador wrote a cable to the State Department that said, "The Clark government's overly strong reaction suggests it sees this flap as an opportunity to bolster its credibility in the Arab world." Thus Mossad's passport scheme fell victim to the sheep-export wars as well as to its own carelessness.

The Israeli government eventually made a very public and uncommonly humble apology for violating New Zealand sovereignty in such a brazen manner. They privately promised Helen Clark they would never again attempt to procure or use false New Zealand passports.

In due course, the prisoners were released, each having served three months of their six-month sentence. They were forced to make a NZ$50,000 donation to Parassist as a condition of their release. The Israeli ambassador eventually returned to his post.

But the black mark would be deeply felt in New Zealand, especially by the Jewish community, for some time. In the midst of the highly publicized trial of Banjo's two family members, vandals daubed swastikas on tombstones in Wellington's historic Jewish cemetery and were never caught.

When I was called upon in a number of subsequent public forums to explain New Zealand's Jewish community's ties to Israel, the charge of "dual loyalty" always hung in the background. In response to the charge, I drew upon what I call the John F. Kennedy defense.

The John F. Kennedy defense first came about during the US presidential campaign of 1960. I wasn't quite mature enough to be politically aware at the time, but when I read about it later, I wholeheartedly took it on board.

John Kennedy was the first Roman Catholic to run for president, and he was asked about the charge of dual loyalty.

In his case, the question was, "If elected president, will you follow the dictates of the Vatican or the Constitution of the United States?" Kennedy's response, which put the question to rest for all time was, "I have a mother and a father, and I love them both."

Jewish New Zealanders have a love for New Zealand and, by and large, a deep affection for Israel—in much the same way as a New Zealander of Italian extraction, for example, would feel affection for the ancestral homeland as well as New Zealand. We all have a mother and a father. We can love them both, equally, at all times.

Drawing upon this logic at the forums, I'd like to think it helped defuse the situation to some degree and that I did my part to enable New Zealand's Jews to get back on an even keel with their neighbors. But despite valiant efforts to bring things right again, some damage had been done.

"Damn those Israelis," I complained to Linda in private. "They can be so arrogant. They don't seem to care about the effect of their actions on diaspora Jewish communities."

"Yes, that may be true, dear," Linda responded. "But they don't *try* to get caught, of course. They just need to be more careful."

"No," I insisted. "They need to stop. Period! And we need to let them know the effect of their actions on us," I added emphatically.

I decided then and there that my next group tour to Israel would be a leadership tour. I would call together twenty leaders of the New Zealand Jewish community and insist that the Israeli embassy make certain we would meet with Israeli leaders, from the prime minister to the minister of defense to the foreign minister. We would tell them face-to-face in no uncertain terms to consider the consequences of their actions.

The brief seven-day Israel visit that followed did have its lighter moments, though. Because we had all been there before—some of us many times—our driver-guide took us off the beaten paths. We went up into the Golan Heights and down into the Negev desert, around some steep bends, and over some high mountain passes. Those of us sitting on the precipitous side of hairpin mountain turns would hold our breath when the driver seemed to dangle his outer tires out over the abyss. Fortunately, we ended up safely in Jerusalem.

As we pulled into the city, the driver stopped the bus, turned to me in front of the group, and said, "I've been watching you, Rabbi, and I must say that I'm a better rabbi than you."

"Why would you say that?" I asked, convinced he wouldn't want to jeopardize our goodwill by making some offensive comment.

"Well," he said, "when you get up to lead people in prayer, they fall asleep. But when I drive my bus, people pray."

We all laughed, of course, especially when he offered the punch line with a good-natured smile.

As we might have expected, we were never given access to all the high-ranking officials we had insisted on seeing in Israel. But we did see some of them.

When we met with the deputy minister of foreign affairs, for example, we told him in no uncertain terms: "Sir, you may not have anticipated the anger of the New Zealand people when you attempted to obtain New Zealand passports illegally. Israel has committed a hostile and shameful act against a long-term friend. If other countries suspect New Zealand passport holders might be Mossad spies, it will cause a great deal of trouble for innocent New Zealand citizens traveling abroad. Do you know that from now on, any of us traveling to Israel will have to undergo the third degree when we come back to New Zealand? What kind of friend are you to do something like this? Your apparent willingness to abuse the trust and confidence of New Zealand suggests that you take our country's friendship for granted. Don't! And don't take us—the Jews of New Zealand—for granted either!"

The minister argued that the passport caper had to do with matters of life and death for Israel; compared to that, what was a little inconvenience for the Jews of New Zealand?

"Find another way to carry out your missions," we told him crossly.

We repeated our appeal to every official we met, even though, as I suspect, our pleas most likely fell on deaf ears. But I'm pretty sure that false New Zealand passports will never again be used by any agency of the State of Israel.

In a few years' time, Mossad's objective behind the New Zealand passport fiasco would become fully transparent. In a few years' time, my old friend Bassem ibn Talal would be in a position to unmask Benjamin "Banjo" Braham in a virtual encounter that I, by pure chance, would play a small part in arranging.

CHAPTER XXIV.

 AUCKLAND. JANUARY 2007.

And there was evening, and there was morning, one day.

Genesis 1:5

Auckland, New Zealand, has more boats per capita than any other city in the world. Children there learn to sail at about the same age as American kids start playing little league. By the time they're in the sixth grade, Kiwi kids are already racing their own P Class sailboats. It's no wonder that major America's Cup yacht race competitors eagerly pursue New Zealand sailors to crew their high-tech yachts; competitive sailing is in the DNA of virtually every native-born New Zealander.

Team New Zealand, to no one's surprise, won the Cup in 1995 and held it until 2003, when a team from Switzerland (comprised of several Kiwis) beat them. New Zealand's next chance to take the Cup back would begin in April 2007 so throughout the southern summer of 2006–07, Team New Zealand yacht crews could be seen practicing for the big challenge in the Hauraki Gulf, near the entrance to Auckland Harbour.

Linda and I had learned to sail in San Francisco Bay, and we still loved being on the water, where, for some reason, I never got seasick. We soon learned that yachting fever, as it is known Down Under, is highly contagious, and virtually everyone residing in New Zealand catches it. We certainly fell under its spell and counted ourselves among the lucky ones fortunate enough to reside in Auckland during those memorable years when New Zealand held the America's Cup.

"My cousin Morris is coming to town next week, Rabbi," congregant Philip Newland reported to me in January 2007. "He's the cruise rabbi on the *Royal Adelaide*, and they'll be docking in Auckland for two full days as part of their world voyage. Morris and the missus are sailing enthusiasts, so we're planning to take them out on the Hauraki Gulf to watch Team New Zealand get ready for the Cup challenge. You're invited if you'd like to come along—I'm sure he'd like to meet you."

Rabbi Morris Leavitt—a retired rabbi from Long Beach, California—was one of, at most, a handful of retired rabbis privileged enough to be placed as cruise rabbis aboard a world cruise. I was on the verge of entering my sixtieth year of life and focusing on 2008 as a potential retirement date, so I jumped at the opportunity to pump Morris Leavitt for all the information he could provide about the life of a cruise rabbi.

"It's rare to be chosen for the full round-the-world voyage," Leavitt told me first off. "But on the other hand, the good news is that most cruise lines take rabbis aboard for shorter voyages during the major Jewish holidays, like Passover, Rosh Hashanah, Yom Kippur, and sometimes Hanukkah. Though we are a very, very small percentage of the world's population, our people do like to travel, as you know, and they do like to celebrate the major holidays with a rabbi, no matter where they are. The cruise lines, I'm pleased to say, are most accommodating. I can give you the name of my agent," he offered. "When you're ready to sail, let me know, and I'll recommend you to her."

Hot dog! I figured to myself. *That's what I'll do in retirement!*

The opportunity was too good to pass up, so I dutifully contacted the agent and sent in the requested résumé accompanied by a cover letter and a tuxedoed photo of myself. I expressed my eagerness to serve at the very next opportunity—even before retirement, if it could be arranged. In fact, I inquired whether it would be possible to be placed as the cruise rabbi aboard the *Southern Dawn* for its Auckland-to-Venice voyage.

Prior to sending my application, Linda and I had searched the Internet and discovered a wonderful calendrical coincidence. The first day of Passover that year would fall on Monday, April 2. In what I playfully described as a perfectly timed, divinely ordained stroke of luck, the Seaboard Cruise Line's *Southern Dawn* was due to set sail out of Auckland that very day, destined for the Middle East and then on to Europe.

Because Passover would begin the night before (as it was for all Jewish holidays, based on Genesis 1:5), we would hold our APHC community Seder the evening of Sunday, April 1, fulfilling my Passover responsibilities. So Linda and I would be free to board the *Southern Dawn* in Viaduct Harbour on April 2.

After sending my application with details of this "divine calendrical coincidence" to Morris's agent, I received, to my surprise, an acceptance letter with *Southern Dawn* boarding passes for Linda and myself, along with a ton of paperwork.

My shipboard duties would be minimal. The ship was scheduled to sail out of Auckland at 5:00 p.m., and I would be expected to conduct a Seder that evening on our way to Sydney. I planned to bring along my own Haggadah booklets, even though Morris had assured me that all the cruise ships carry their own books for Jewish and Christian services and celebrations. For the remaining seven days of the festival, I would need to ensure that certain Passover foods, such as kosher wine and matzah, were available upon request. Each Friday night, I would be expected to conduct a Sabbath service. And throughout the cruise, I would be required to be on hand in my official role of "guest lecturer" to schmooze and counsel as necessary.

Having been chosen as the cruise rabbi started the secular New Year Down Under off on an auspicious beginning for me. Now all I needed to do was wait eagerly for April 2.

But what I did not know at the time was that our maiden voyage would turn out to be more than a mere pleasure cruise. That reality began to come to light later that month, after news from Dubai grabbed headlines around the world. In the middle of it all would be my old friend Bassem ibn Talal, now head of general security for the Emirate of Dubai.

CHAPTER XXV:

 AUCKLAND. JANUARY 2007.

He who seeks revenge should remember to dig two graves.

CHINESE PROVERB

MIDEAST ARMS DEALER ASSASSINATED IN DUBAI HOTEL.
The headline from Dubai first hit the *New Zealand Post*
and other major newspapers on January 29, ten days after the
incident.

I did not recognize the victim's name at first—Mahmoud
al-Mugrabi—but I knew the story. In 1989, al-Mugrabi and another terrorist disguised as Orthodox Jews stopped their car at a
popular Israeli transit spot and picked up two hitchhiking Israeli
soldiers. After murdering the soldiers and mutilating their bodies,
they buried them just inside the Gaza Strip.

For this and other murderous acts with which I was not familiar, al-Mugrabi—a life member of the Muslim Brotherhood
and founder of the Kassem Brigade terrorist group—was a "most
wanted" man not only by the Israelis but by the Egyptian and
Jordanian secret services as well. All three sought to bring him
to justice—or "bring justice to him." In the intervening years, he
survived more than one assassination attempt.

To set aside all doubt about the soldiers' murder, al-Mugrabi made a video broadcast on the Voice of Palestine television station. He publicly admitted his involvement—celebrated it, in fact—in the murder and mutilation of the two Israeli soldiers. He described the act in graphic detail. That broadcast in all likelihood sealed his final death warrant. He would be dead two weeks later.

Al-Mugrabi had gone to Dubai on an arms-procurement mission. He flew in from Damascus, using one of the five different false passports found in his hotel room. He checked into the five-star Al-Quds Hotel at 3:05 p.m. on January 19, requesting a room with sealed windows and no balcony. He left the hotel about an hour after check-in. No one knows what he did or where he went during the next four hours.

During his long absence, various assassination team members wearing baseball caps pulled down over their eyes entered al-Mugrabi's room and waited for him to return. Hotel computer logs indicated that an attempt was made to reprogram his electronic door lock during this period.

At approximately 8:25 p.m., al-Mugrabi returned to his room. He failed to answer a phone call from his wife a half hour later. When a hotel maid tried to enter his room the next morning, she found the door locked from the inside. Hearing no response from inside, she alerted hotel authorities, who broke into the room and found al-Mugrabi lying in his bed, a bottle of prescription medicine on the bedside table.

Initially, Dubai authorities believed the man—his true identity still unknown—had died of natural causes. But taking into consideration the time he had returned to his room and the unanswered phone call, they determined the time of his death as between 8:30 and 9:00 p.m. And then they began to ask questions. A subsequent autopsy revealed that the victim had been injected with a paralyzing drug called succinylcholine and then suffocated with his pillow.

Three days after the murder, Police Chief Bassem ibn Talal received a phone call from Kassem Brigade headquarters in Damascus, reporting that their arms agent, Mahmoud al-Mugrabi, had gone missing in Dubai. They admitted he had used a false passport to achieve entry into the country, and they apologized to ibn Talal for not having informed him of the visit. That's how Bassem learned the man's real identity. He was furious.

"Take yourselves and your bank accounts and your weapons and your forged fucking passports, and get out of my country!" the livid ibn Talal reportedly shouted at the Kassem Brigade man.

While ibn Talal may have been unable to prevent the killing, at least he could get some compensation for the violation of his state's sovereignty by launching a massive criminal investigation. And he would ensure that the investigation itself would become a personal triumph: lieutenant general and head of general security for the Emirate of Dubai, Minister Bassem ibn Talal, the supercop of Dubai—and graduate of the criminal justice department of North Bay State University, North Bay, California!

He began by sorting through 648 hours of video footage that had been pieced together from various surveillance cameras posted throughout Dubai, including the hotel and airport.

At first, the Dubai police would not believe it was a Mossad job. Mossad, as conventional wisdom would have it, was much cleverer than that, despite the New Zealand fiasco and other missteps. Would the Israelis have been so stupid as to allow themselves to be caught on camera? Would they not have known that American-trained ibn Talal had ordered twenty-five thousand surveillance cameras installed throughout Dubai—at every port of entry, on every major thoroughfare, in every residential tower, in every hotel, in every shopping center, and in every public building?

Furthermore, an investigation revealed that two Palestinians, members of a rival faction, had provided logistical support to the assassination team. This fact cast further doubt on a possible Mossad connection. Would the Israelis have employed agents of their sworn enemy, the Palestinians?

Another curious aspect was that two of the "suspects," as the Dubai police called the assassins, were reported to have gotten away by tourist ferry across the Persian Gulf to Iran. If it was, indeed, an Israeli operation, the last place its secret agents would want to escape to was Iran.

So how could it have been an Israeli operation? Was it not obvious to all that they were not the only ones interested in having al-Mugrabi murdered? Could it have been a rival Palestinian faction? An Egyptian hit? Jordanian? Perhaps even a Shi'ite group from Iran?

On February 16, ibn Talal called a press conference. Reporters from around the world gathered in his office at Dubai police headquarters on Beirut Road. He then showed a craftily prepared thirty-minute video of the entire assassination operation, covering the

181

arrival of the assassins, through the arrival of al-Mugrabi, to the assassination team's departure. The video was a Hollywood-quality production, complete with subtitles and a time-indicator clock.

It was then posted on a new video website called YouTube and shown to an international audience said to number forty million. The subtitles narrated the story, and as each assassination team suspect appeared in the video, the name he or she used to enter Dubai was displayed.

The surveillance evidence had helped ibn Talal match faces on the Al-Quds hotel tapes to passport photos the assassination team had used. As it turned out, they had entered Dubai on various Australian, British, Dutch, French, German, and Irish passports. When it was discovered, however, that seven of the eleven passports were false passports issued in the names of Israeli citizens possessing dual nationality, suspicions began to focus on Israel in earnest.

Within a few hours of Bassem's press conference, the news wires lit up with reports of outraged men and women in Israel, the United Kingdom, Ireland, France, and Germany, claiming their identities had been stolen and used by the eleven perpetrators of the al-Mugrabi murder. There was so much international flak that Interpol secretary general Ronald Welborn soon declared that because these passports had been fraudulently obtained, Interpol would clear the names of the innocent citizens whose identities had been stolen.

Israel's deputy minister of foreign affairs, Daniel Kidron, quickly denied that Israel was behind the killing in Dubai or that this situation would damage Israeli-European relations.

"There is nothing linking Israel to the assassination of al-Mugrabi," Kidron said at an event in Haifa.

It was true. No hard evidence could be produced.

"Britain, Germany, and France are partners to the ongoing struggle against global terrorism, so I'm certain there won't be a crisis," the deputy minister of foreign affairs concluded.

Along with the denials came blame. A Hamas legislator stated that the Kassem Brigade founder was himself to blame by booking his trip through the Internet. The same legislator also told a news conference that the slain man took an additional risk by informing his Gaza family by telephone about the hotel where he was staying. Hamas also claimed that two ex-officers from their rival faction, the PLO, had been involved in al-Mugrabi's assassination. The PLO shot back by insinuating that Hamas members had collaborated with the killers.

On February 20, ibn Talal called a second press conference, where he showed a further twelve-minute video from the surveillance tapes and accompanied it with his verbal narrative.

Toward the end of his account, he added, "There were no traces left behind at the murder scene to help uncover the real identities of the perpetrators of this crime. However, our investigation is ongoing. If you can identify any of the faces you will now see on your screen, please contact me, Police Chief Bassem ibn Talal, at the Dubai Security Services Office. We are offering a generous reward. Detailed contact information can be found on our website."

Over the next few minutes, the photos of all eleven people believed to be involved in the murder of al-Mugrabi were shown on the screen. The photos of the three individuals deemed the organizers and directors of the operation were also posted separately on the Dubai police website, under the heading "Most Wanted."

We watched the incredible news unfold in our living room in Devonport, fully aware that Linda and I would soon be actually in Dubai, a major port on our cruise itinerary. I recorded both surveillance videos on our VCR so I could watch them more carefully again. I was relieved to learn that the suspects had not used one New Zealand passport during the operation.

As gruesome as the story was, I had to admit to Linda that I felt a certain degree of pride as we watched our friend Bassem ibn Talal strut his stuff in front of such a vast worldwide audience. I remembered how Bassem had once helped us defuse what could have been a very explosive situation back in 1991, when the Aryan Woodstock group came into town.

I wondered, would the perpetrators of this extrajudicial assassination ever be identified with any degree of certainty? I also had to question, had Israeli intelligence lost its touch? Did it get stuck somewhere back in the late twentieth century? And could Banjo Braham possibly have had a hand in what now appeared to be yet another Mossad screw-up?

That's when I decided to take a closer look at those photos flashing across the television screen . . .

CHAPTER XXVI:

 AUCKLAND. FEBRUARY 2007.

Did we keep silent when we should have spoken out?

RABBI SIDNEY GREENBERG

"Look at that! Look at that!" I shouted to Linda as we watched Bassem ibn Talal's latest video in our Devonport living room. Our VCR had recorded the entire presentation. "Look at that! That's him. That's Banjo Braham, coming through that hotel door. He's shaved his head, but it's him!"

Linda came over to watch with me.

"Now look," I said. "He goes into the men's room and comes out with a mustache, a full head of hair, and glasses. That's Benjamin Braham. Now we know what he was up to last year. That must be why he disappeared."

But could I prove it? And would I want to, given al-Mugrabi's horrific deeds? And would I dare to, considering the long arm of the Mossad?

A line from our High Holy Day prayer book began to rumble through my mind: "Did we keep silent when we should have spoken out?" That passage has always spoken to me. But now I had to consider, what about the risks? And what about the possible damage to Israel? Was I seeking to help an old friend or harm an old adversary? Was I looking to bring some measure of justice to Benjamin Braham, or was it just artless vengeance that I sought?

I was clearly at a crossroads now, caught on the horns of a dilemma. So I decided to talk to my rabbi. I picked up the phone and called my colleague and mentor, Rabbi Matthew Isaacson in Wellington.

"Matthew," I said, "I'm having a bit of a spiritual crisis, and I hope you can help."

I didn't want to name any names nor reveal too many details. I told him I knew a kind of "unsavory character" who had done some "troublesome" things in the past. I was now fairly certain he was involved in a crime. I couldn't prove it, but I could identify him to someone who would be in a position to bring him to justice.

So I told him, "It all boils down to one question: Should I keep silent, or should I speak out?"

I could hear him scribbling notes.

"I see," he said. "I see. I see. Let me have a little think about all this. I'll call you back."

About two hours later, my phone rang. It was Matthew.

"Okay," he said, "without knowing any of the particulars, I would say it's not up to you to try to effect justice. That's why we have courts of law. And although no one seems to have enough evidence to bring anyone to court, God has many agents through whom he can work."

"So," I asked him, "if an agent is asking for help, can I go ahead and give him some assistance? I mean, if we wait for God to act, it could take a long time!"

"Ah, there's the catch-22!" he replied. "On the one hand, we have 'Do not go out as a talebearer among your people.' On the other hand, 'nor shall you endanger the life of your neighbor' by holding your tongue. And that entire paradox is contained within a single biblical verse, Leviticus 19:16! So I would say that part of not 'endangering' is to let 'your neighbor' know about your past experience, in order to prevent the troublesome behavior from recurring out in the world."

That was all I needed to hear.

"Thank you, Matthew," I finally said. "That's very helpful, indeed. I think I can see now what I need to do."

Then a clear sign came to me. The summer weather Down Under drew Mark Dixon, PhD—professor in the School of Electronics and Computer Science at the University of Northampton, England—back to his hometown of Auckland. Dixon had come to deliver a lecture entitled "Forget Fingerprints: How Scotland Yard Found Martin Luther King's Assassin" at the University of Auckland. I was keen to attend the lecture after reading the *New Zealand Post* announcement touting the professor's "significant contribution to the field of forensic science."

I arrived early and took careful notes as the professor spoke to a small audience at University Hall. Dixon claimed that our ears are more secure from the effects of aging than other facial features are. They also can be recognized from a distance. His method could scan a person's ear from an early photograph and compare it to a later photograph or even a clear video. He went on to explain that his ear-identification system was a great improvement upon an earlier system used in 1960 to positively identify the infamous Adolf Eichmann before his capture by the Mossad. Scotland Yard used the same earlier method to identify James Earl Ray, the notorious assassin of the Reverend Dr. Martin Luther King. He was caught in London at Heathrow Airport in 1968.

"With facial-recognition technology, on the other hand," he explained, "a lot of the problems happen when people get old. Crow's feet and other signs of aging confuse the biometric systems. Your ears, however, age very gracefully. They grow proportionally larger, and your lobe gets a bit more elongated, it is true. But otherwise your ears remain fully formed from birth. The ears do not experience significant changes over a lifetime."

Spurred on by Dixon's remarks, I rushed back home to see what photos I had of Banjo Braham.

"Linda! Linda!" I called out as I slammed our street-level door behind me and ran up the private stairway to our second-floor flat. "How do I retrieve those photos from last year's Purim celebration?"

"They're in iPhoto on the computer," she called to me from our living room as I entered the apartment. "Just open up iPhoto."

I ran to the computer. "Okay—that much I can do. But is it possible to print a hard copy of a digital photo?"

"Yes, it's possible, but I'd have to walk you through the steps. You're a bit of a Luddite, you know, darlin'."

With Linda standing over me to supervise my moves, I found what I was looking for. It was a color photograph of "Ben Skooler" from his brief sojourn in Auckland, before the passport debacle. I had taken it during the Purim celebration for which Banjo and his Community Guardian Group trainees provided security. It was a profile shot clearly showing the right side of Banjo's head as he gazed upon the crowd. He had waved me off when he heard the shutter click.

No photos—no wonder! Now I knew why. But I had my one photo. And then, sure enough, I found another shot of him in the crowd, taken from a distance.

"Can I zoom in to feature him head on?"

"Yes, but you'll lose some quality," Linda responded. She guided me through the editing process.

"Now what do I do?" I asked her. "How can I make these into prints?"

Linda once again guided me, this time through the process of putting the digital photos onto a flash drive.

"Wow," I said. "It's a miracle."

"No. It's a computer," she retorted. "Welcome to the twenty-first century."

Next, I went to a photo album and drew two pictures of Banjo Braham as a much younger man—color snapshots from our kibbutz men's afternoon tea gatherings, glossy photos with white scalloped borders, decades old but still clear. One was a side shot from the same angle as the Purim photo, and another was a head-on shot from a different day. There were other photographs of my afternoon tea group, but these two shots were the best I had of the younger Banjo.

The next day, I brought the flash drive to the Devonport Print Shop and asked them to make color prints of the digital photos.

Upon my return, I sat down to compose a letter to Dubai's head of general security, my old friend Bassem ibn Talal.

CHAPTER XXVII.

 AUCKLAND. MARCH 2007.

Thy friend has a friend, and thy friend's friend has a friend:
Be discreet.

TALMUD

1 March 2007
Lieutenant General Minister Bassem ibn Talal,
Head of General Security
Department of Protective Services
Dubai Police Headquarters
Al Ittihad Road, Al Twar First
Dubai, United Arab Emirates

Dear Minister ibn Talal,

Merhaba, *Minister ibn Talal. Although many years*
have passed, I hope you remember me as rabbi of the
North Bay Jewish Center while you were in the crimi-
nal justice program at North Bay State University. For
nearly sixteen years, I have wondered how I might pay
you back for the wonderful service you rendered to the

entire North Bay community during the "Aryan Wood-stock" affair. I am currently serving a congregation in Auckland, New Zealand, and I believe I have now found a way to repay you.

I must first of all congratulate you on your fine achievement. The manner in which you investigated the assassination of Mahmoud al-Mugrabi in the Al-Quds hotel on 19 January of this year, and so flawlessly presented your extraordinary findings to the entire world, is exceptional. Certainly you have set the bar quite high in your field. I have been following your career carefully and am fully aware of all your past successes, for which I also congratulate you. I am among your many admirers around the world who regard this most recent triumph as your crowning achievement, which I hope you agree it is. And perhaps I can help in the investigation.

I have recently uncovered vital information I believe will enable you to apprehend a leader—perhaps the leader—of the group responsible for the al-Mugrabi assassination. The image of this man appears on the "Most Wanted" screen on your Dubai State Security website. I have in my possession other photographs of him to assist you in proving his identity.

As it turns out, my wife, Linda, and I will arrive in Dubai, inshallah, *on 24 April this year aboard the Seaboard Cruise Line's* Southern Dawn. *Perhaps you and I can meet in your office that day or the next morning to discuss this matter more fully.*

I hesitate to use e-mail for this communication due to obvious security concerns. I believe we should, rather, communicate exclusively by regular post and face-to-face meetings, hence this letter. Please, therefore, kindly write to me, Rabbi Jonathan Kadison, at the following address:

25978 Calliope Road
Devonport, Auckland
New Zealand

Thank you very much for your consideration, dear Minister ibn Talal.

Yours in peace,
Rabbi Jonathan Kadison

***

23 March 2007

Dear Rabbi Kadison,

I am very happy to hear that you will be arriving in Dubai on 24 April. Please do come to my office, on the third floor of Dubai Police Headquarters.

As your cruise ship docks at 8:00 a.m., shall we set our meeting for 2:00 p.m. that Tuesday afternoon? I am hoping that will give you and your wife ample time to explore our wonderful and prosperous city.

I look forward to seeing you then, inshallah.

Maa tahiyati,
Bassem
Minister Bassem ibn Talal

As I held his letter in my hands, the sixteen years melted away. I was thrilled to be remembered by someone who now strode so prominently upon the world stage.

Yet my excitement was tempered by a growing sense of apprehension. Who was I to meddle in this murky world of espionage and criminal justice? In my own eyes, I was still a small country-town rabbi, one of many thousands worldwide.

But the friendly tone of the letter and the fact that he signed it "Bassem" in his own hand gave me courage. With his warm response, I knew our maiden voyage on the *Southern Dawn* would transform into something more than a working holiday. I was a now man with a mission.

The month of March flew by as we prepared for Passover. Our portion of the cruise was to begin in Auckland and continue on to Sydney, Bali, Singapore, Phuket, Mumbai, and Dubai. Once we arrived in Dubai, our duties would be fulfilled, with Passover well over. Linda and I would be allowed to overnight aboard the *Southern Dawn* in Port Rashid in Dubai, then we'd disembark by noon the next day—day twenty-four of the thirty-seven-day itinerary. We were scheduled to fly home to Auckland via Singapore that evening while the *Southern Dawn* continued its voyage to Venice.

In preparation for my meeting with Bassem, I studied the city of Dubai quite extensively. I pored over street maps borrowed and copied from the Auckland Central City Library. I zoomed in on Dubai Police Headquarters on Google Earth. I carefully calculated the distance from the police headquarters to the passenger terminal at Port Rashid. I decided that, given enough time before sunset, I would walk back through the historic Bastakiya neighborhood and the famous Old Souk following the meeting.

On April 2, 2007, the day following the Auckland Progressive Hebrew Congregation's Sunday evening Seder, we made our way to Viaduct Harbour, where the *Southern Dawn* was docked. It was small by modern cruise ship standards, carrying only 850 passengers, most of whom had paid upwards of $10,000 per person for the voyage.

We were led to our interior cabin, where we found two single beds pushed together, two nightstands, a small sofa with a coffee table, a desk with a large mirror, a comfortable desk chair, a television set, a closet with drawers, and a bathroom with toilet, sink, and shower—all tightly packed into a room no larger than 180 square feet. It was cozy and thoughtfully appointed, but above all it was dark and quiet at night, allowing us many hours to sleep and relax following an intense period of anticipation and preparation.

Once unpacked, I met with Fiona, the assistant cruise director, to prepare for the Seder while the ship was still in port. A few hours later, we set sail for Sydney.

The Seder was advertised in the daily newsletter placed on each bed. Because this was the only advance notice, we didn't expect a large crowd. But to our surprise, forty passengers showed up for the Seder. Some, no doubt, came out of a sense of tradition. Others, I'm certain, came out of curiosity. It turned out to be a joyous celebration, full of singing, storytelling, table-side ceremonies, and an excellent meal prepared by the ship's head chef. That night, the chef told me he had worked at a Jewish resort in Switzerland. He was familiar with the religious requirements of Jewish passengers, and he extended the offer to do anything else he could do to make their voyage comfortable over the holiday period.

The voyage was mostly uneventful for the first nineteen days. But as we departed Mumbai and sailed toward the Persian Gulf, the entire ship underwent a piracy-safety drill. My fellow passengers and I soon learned there were other dangers as well.

When we entered the Persian Gulf, for example, an Iranian patrol boat with twin-mounted .50-caliber machine guns "buzzed" the *Southern Dawn*, rapidly advancing toward the starboard side and then veering off at the last moment. Nothing was said about the feigned attack, but a number of passengers witnessed the maneuver.

I watched it too. It happened just as Leonard, the cruise director, was recording his daily "morning show" on the aft deck. When the prerecorded morning show was broadcast the next morning, discerning viewers noticed that Leonard called for an abrupt "cut" just after he glanced off into the distance. He must have seen the approaching patrol boat because the sudden anxious look on his face told a worried story.

What was also apparent to the discerning passenger—and more than a little comforting—was the presence of the US Navy's Fifth Fleet just over the horizon as we sailed toward Dubai in the Persian Gulf.

We pulled into Dubai's new Port Rashid just as the sun was rising in the east. My private plan was to meet with Bassem twice. The first meeting would be held according to our arrangement at 2:00 p.m. that day. I would present my photographic evidence and explain to Bassem how I had arrived at my conclusions. Before taking my leave, I would invite him to examine my photos scientifically and compare them with his own photographic evidence. If he then wished to proceed, he could call me back for another meeting the next day before our 6:00 p.m. airport departure. At the second meeting I would identify the man in the photos as Benjamin Braham and share the dossier I had prepared.

But first, I would have to do my level best to get us, two old friends from such different worlds, on the same page. I prepared myself for a mighty effort.

CHAPTER XXVIII.

 DUBAI. APRIL 2007.

Vengeance is not the point; change is.

BARBARA DEMING

At Bassem's suggestion, Linda and I spent the first part of the day touring Dubai on foot. We were glad we had gotten off to an early start, as by 1:00 in the afternoon, the temperature had already soared to eighty-nine degrees.

It was an important part of our plan to have Linda safely aboard the ship during the first meeting—just in case. So an hour before my scheduled meeting, Linda hopped in a taxi to ride back to Port Rashid.

Carrying my sport coat over my shoulder now, I headed at a leisurely pace toward Dubai Police Headquarters, stopping to rest in the shade as much as possible.

Despite our shore excursion manager's assurances of "absolute safety" in Dubai, I was a bit apprehensive when I arrived at the police headquarters. It was not exactly an ordinary stop on the typical tourist route. I was able to walk in off the street, to be sure. But I had to be buzzed in past a guard from the small tiled entrance lobby, which was surrounded by thick bulletproof glass.

The guard patted me down and then dutifully checked my black briefcase, which carried everything I needed. This included my New Zealand passport (which I now carried along with my American passport for international travel), my Seaboard passenger identity card, my driver's license, and some cash and credit cards. It also held family photos; carefully placed among them were two slightly frayed snapshots of the men's tea from my kibbutz days and the more recent photographs of "Ben Skooler" in Auckland. Plus, there was the flash drive from which these prints had been made and my notes from Dr. Dixon's lecture. The complete dossier on Benjamin Braham was back aboard the *Southern Dawn*, under Linda's watchful eye.

When I informed the guard that I had a 2:00 p.m. appointment with Minister Bassem ibn Talal, the guard spoke into his jacket lapel. As I peered through the bulletproof glass, I noticed someone behind a counter on the other side responding to the guard—or so it seemed—on her headset.

Once inside, I spoke briefly to the woman with the headset, who then gestured toward the elegant stairway at the end of the inner lobby. In a stern voice, she said only, "Room 301."

But when I glanced toward the stairway, I saw that half of this inner lobby, including the entire counter area and the desks behind it, was enclosed in a kind of wire cage about eight feet high. The woman called to a man seated at a desk on the other side of the cage. The man then walked over to the cage door, situated about ten feet in front of the stairway. He unlocked it and held it open for me. I walked through the cage door, nodding in gratitude toward him. Feigning nonchalance, I began to walk up the stairway.

I was certain that every move I made was being watched. As I placed my foot upon the first step, a strange thing happened: two young men dressed in suits came out of nowhere to accompany me on my ascent.

I tried to make no outward sign of panic, but I told myself in a silent monologue, *I know where I've felt like this before. It was just outside Damascus Gate. In Jerusalem. When I walked outside that gate, a swarm of young men closed in on me. When I told them I was going to the American consulate, they faded away—thank God. But this is not East Jerusalem. It's a police station. I'm safe here. Right?*

When we reached the third floor, the young suited men guided me to a desk outside an elaborately carved wooden door. They stood nearby and watched as I approached the secretary, who took my name and asked me to be seated inside.

Once through the door, I found myself in a spacious waiting room with tiled flooring and comfortable lounge chairs. Evidently, I was the only one scheduled to see the police chief that afternoon. As I took a seat, I smiled nervously at another secretary, who was seated at a desk in front of yet another door, this one wood paneled. The two young men also took their seats, one next to me and one opposite.

After about forty-five minutes, the secretary told me, "You may see the minister now, sir," as she gestured toward the wood-paneled door behind her. The two guards remained in their seats.

When I entered his office, Bassem was already standing at his desk, resplendent in his military uniform. He came out from behind the desk and grasped my right hand with his own. I was relieved to receive a warm greeting.

"*Assalamu alaikum*, Minister Bassem," I said anxiously as I presented him with a gift. It was a wooden letter opener with a Maori carving on the handle. I also presented my business card, careful to hold it with both hands and bow slightly as I held it out for him—all according to custom.

"*Wa alaikum assalam*, Rabbi Jonathan. Thank you," came the response.

Bassem was no longer a young graduate student; that much was readily apparent. The officer standing before me was now a middle-aged man, still mustachioed, whose black hair had become unevenly salt-and-peppered.

I, on the other hand, was now a senior citizen on the verge of retirement, although often told I looked younger than my age. My sideburns had become almost completely white, but the rest of my head of hair showed only random strands of gray.

"You look well," Bassem said.

"Thank you, Minister Bassem. But as you would understand, I've grown gray at the Temples."

We both chuckled over one of my favorite puns.

"And the years have been good to you as well, my friend," I replied. "How is your family?"

After exchanging a few more pleasantries, we sat down on opposite sides of Bassem's massive desk as I began my well-prepared presentation.

"Minister Bassem," I proceeded in a rather deferential manner befitting the occasion as well as my respect for the man and his position. This was not a time for chitchat. "I am deeply grateful for this meeting. I will never forget the favor you did my community and me during the Aryan Woodstock incident. I have been looking—all these years—for an opportunity to return your kindness, and such an opportunity has recently fallen into my lap."

"There is no need for that, Rabbi," the security chief politely responded. "I believe your own tradition says, 'A good deed is its own reward.' The Koran says something very similar."

"'Whatever you do of good deeds, truly Allah knows it well,'" I quoted.

It was a Koranic passage with which I was happily familiar. It elicited a smile from Bassem. Then I continued in the same respectful manner.

"But I have in my possession what I believe is evidence of the real identity of one of the principal perpetrators of the assassination of Mahmoud al-Mugrabi. Before I wrote to you, I attended a lecture by Professor Mark Dixon, and his words gave me the inspiration to find and present to you evidence that I hope will help you identify the man. I further believe that this man was one of the leaders, if not *the* ringleader, of the entire operation.

"I do not have proof—only a reasonable assumption—that the operation was an Israeli undertaking. But I can tell you that I have known this man for more than three decades. I know he has worked for Israeli intelligence. My only desire is to ask you to look at the evidence I offer today, compare it with the evidence you already have, and draw your own conclusions.

"This man's false passport photograph, I believe, is one of the three that appear on your website under the 'Most Wanted' heading. He has shaved his head and has aged somewhat. But"—I paused as I opened my briefcase, pulled out the color snapshots of my kibbutz tea group, leaned over the desk, and presented them to Bassem—"I am confident he is in these photographs."

"Hmm," Bassem muttered pensively as he examined the kibbutz photos. "These are very old photographs. The man in these photos is much younger than any of the three on our website." He sounded more than a little incredulous.

I paused again, remembering my strategy to invite him to draw his own conclusions one step at a time. In preparation for this meeting, Linda and I had agreed that I needed to respectfully defer to Bassem and offer nothing more than my humble assistance. We were convinced that only his imprimatur would bring about the intended result, that only he had the tools, the ability, and the motivation to connect the dots.

"Well," I said as I reached into my briefcase to retrieve the digital prints, "as evidence of his current appearance, I have these more recent photographs. I'm happy to also give you a flash drive so you will be one generation closer to the original photos, taken just over a year ago, when this man was in my Auckland community. Does he not resemble one of your three 'Most Wanted'?"

"Resemble, perhaps," Bassem answered, sounding a bit unconvinced.

"I apologize, Minister Bassem, if I cannot provide you with absolute proof at this point. I have come before you today with the humble intention of presenting these photographs to assist in your investigation. I am hoping that you have similar video captures of the man and can connect the dots, so to speak. The simple, very elementary understanding of forensic science I acquired from Professor Dixon's lecture is that there is a way to apply various scientific tools to prove the identity of a person from photographs. My hope is that you can authenticate what is, for me, hardly more than a layman's guess that these photographs and the photo on your website are of the same person."

I tried to be as unassuming as possible, taking into account Bassem's probable natural—and well-justified—suspicion of my methods and motives.

While Bassem continued to look casually at the photographs, I spoke up again. "My ship will be in port, as you know, until late tomorrow. My wife and I are to disembark at noon. Perhaps you can send a message to me if you wish to proceed, and we can set up another meeting. I have no obligations tomorrow before we depart by airplane at 6:00 p.m. We can even meet nearby at the airport, if you wish." We could see the planes taking off and landing from his office window.

"But above all, take your time. Please have your experts examine the evidence carefully. Once you are confident that these photos and the video captures from your own surveillance cameras are of one and the same man, we can meet again and I can tell you everything I know about him."

I was thinking, of course, about the dossier I had prepared in anticipation of a follow-up meeting with Bassem.

Bassem nodded, though I couldn't tell for certain if he was accepting anything I was trying to convey.

"And why do you think this may be an Israeli operation?" he asked at long last.

"Thank you for allowing me to explain. First, I believe that Israeli intelligence underestimated you—your exceptional talent, the education you obtained in the criminal justice department at North Bay State, as well as your considerable professional abilities. When you rose to your present position, it was obvious to many that you had an elaborate system of security cameras placed in every hotel, in every shopping center, on the streets, in the hallways of every major building, and at every transportation hub in Dubai. But it wasn't obvious to the Israelis."

"We had twenty-five thousand cameras at the time. Soon we'll have one hundred thousand," Bassem proudly added.

I could tell my deferential words were finally beginning to have their anticipated effect.

"That's brilliant!" I said before continuing with my reasoning. "Second, it is true that other countries wanted al-Mugrabi dead, but I would argue, none as much as Israel.

"Third, it is also true that two members of the assassination team escaped by tourist ferry to the Iranian port of Bandar Abbas, lending credence to the argument that no Israeli would have gone in *that* direction. But if you will allow me, I believe I can explain that one to you. I witnessed with my own eyes the New Zealand passport scandal—in which, by the way, I believe this man was involved. But Australia also does a brisk trade with Iran. You know better than I that Australian and New Zealand nationals—that is, those who present those countries' passports, however acquired," I added with an exaggerated wink, "can obtain an Iranian tourist visa under their Visa On Arrival program."

Bassem smiled a knowing smile. He had probably already arrived at the same conclusion about the Iranian ferry puzzle. A number of Australian passports had been used in the Al-Quds assassination enterprise.

"Fourth and finally, General Meir Tirosh, the head of Mossad, resigned—as you know—on March 30. His resignation was so discreet that it received only scant attention in the media. I believe he was forced out, but only after enough time had elapsed so as not to raise the suspicion that his resignation had anything to do with operational blunders here in Dubai."

"I can see you have given this matter a great deal of thought, Rabbi." Bassem was beginning to warm up to my presentation. "But there is one very obvious question I must ask: What is your motivation in all of this? You want to return me a favor, yes. But in this way? After all, it goes without saying that you are an American rabbi. Though now serving in New Zealand, you are an American rabbi who is a member of a group among the most vocal supporters of Israel."

"Yes, Bassem—may I call you Bassem?"

He nodded. "Of course."

Deference, I knew, was an important part of Middle Eastern culture. But Bassem had been educated in America—in California, in fact—so I was hoping first-name informality might be acceptable at this point in our discussion.

"What you say is mostly true." I was prepared for this. Linda had posed the same challenge. "However, you may remember from our discussions some years ago that we don't all believe that Israel can do no wrong, that it's 'my ancestral homeland, right or wrong!'

"And even if I did believe that, this is not so much about Israel, in my opinion, as much as it is about one arrogant man. A man who, through his involvement in the New Zealand passport scandal, brought dishonor to my Auckland community, apparently without so much as a second thought as to the consequences of his actions and their impact upon us. Also, this same man, due to his own incompetence, allowed my best friend to be killed on the Golan Heights battlefield and was never tried for it. In addition, he once led a vendetta against me personally."

"So," Bassem answered in a slightly accusatory tone, "this is about revenge! Is that it?"

"That is certainly part of the story," I admitted. "But I would say, dear friend, it is more about *justice*. I am hoping that, should you be interested in pursuing this matter further, you will issue an arrest warrant for him through Interpol, linking your website photograph to his real name—his birth name, the name given to him by his parents. This man has violated your sovereignty and wantonly conducted his activities in my own community with callous disregard. This man is, in my opinion, a murderer!"

My voice was rising now, as if I were back in the pulpit. I was angry because I was thinking of my kibbutz buddy, Michael. I told myself to calm down. I then continued in a slower, quieter voice.

"A man like that deserves to be confined to his own country—trapped in Israel—for the rest of his life. We both know that's the worst that will happen to him, and I believe it is a *just* sentence.

"But there is still more," I added, taking a deep breath.

There was a long pause, an intentional pause, as I wanted what I was about to say to be remembered. My final motivation was as much about the future as about the past. So I spoke very deliberately.

"I believe, along with many others, that Dubai is the symbol of the new Middle East. You and your countrymen have fashioned Dubai into an oasis of peace and prosperity, a hub of worldwide commerce, a place of tolerance and modernity—the Singapore, if you will, of the Arab world. I experienced your progressive entrepreneurial spirit myself at your gorgeous Port Rashid cruise terminal just this morning on my way over here.

"I also believe that Israel needs to integrate itself more fully into the Middle East. It has already made peace with Egypt and Jordan. But I believe the path to its future leads through Dubai and the United Arab Emirates, of which you are a leading member.

"I hope you will expose this as a Mossad operation, even if only through diplomatic channels, and that it results in an apology, even a private one, like the one apparently conveyed to New Zealand. I hope that following such an apology, your government can build on the tentative trade relations you were already establishing with Israel before this year began. Such an outcome would be good for Dubai, good for Israel, and good for the future of the new Middle East. Don't you think? If your investigation results in such an apology, we can write a new chapter with words that will resonate throughout the world."

Bassem nodded and continued to nod even after I had finished my appeal. Then after some time, he drew a deep breath and said, very slowly, "*Inshallah.*"

Our meeting was now clearly over.

"*Im yirtze Hashem,*" I said with a half bow as I shook Bassem's hand.

He escorted me to the door of his office. We shook hands again, and I took my leave.

CHAPTER XXIX.

 AUCKLAND. JUNE 2007.

Justice delayed . . . justice denied.
PIRKEI AVOT: SAYINGS OF THE FATHERS, CHAPTER V

It was late in the afternoon by the time I concluded my meeting with Bassem. The hot Dubai sun was already casting its long shadows. Despite all the assurances of personal safety, I did not relish the thought of meandering at dusk through the labyrinthine Old Souk on my way back to Port Rashid. I decided to skip that part of my walking plan and made my way instead along Dubai Creek, past the old fishing boats, directly to our ship.

When I reached Al Wasl Road, I could see the *Southern Dawn* in the distance, but I discovered that a long fence separated the port area from the road. The fence seemed to stretch along the road for miles. So I hopped in a cab and was driven directly to the ship.

I checked for messages at the purser's desk and discovered none were waiting for me. *Well*, I thought, *it's still the tourist season, and he must be busy with other matters. He's nothing if not a thorough investigator. He just needs a few more hours. I'll check again later and again in the morning if necessary.*

Once back in our room, I added to my briefcase the complete dossier on Benjamin Braham. It included a biographical sketch chronicling his birth date, his birth name, his parents' names, his place of birth, and an account of his early life in Brisbane during the Second World War. I added what I knew of his parents' demise and how I believed it had shaped his attitudes and beliefs. I documented his immigration to Israel, the background of his nickname, his kibbutz work, some of my encounters with him, and his military rank at the time of the Yom Kippur War. I also detailed some of the legends about him and recounted his recent sojourn in New Zealand just before the passport scandal broke out into the open. The entire eight-page profile was contained in a clear blue plastic report cover labeled "Benjamin 'Banjo' Braham."

My intention was to present this evidence to Bassem once he had confirmed that my photographic evidence matched the results of his own investigation, proving that Banjo Braham was involved in the Al-Quds assassination. The information I now carried in my briefcase was all he would need to complete the circle and verify the true identity of a key participant.

That is, if Bassem wished to meet again. I was beginning to have my doubts, especially after checking with the purser one more time after breakfast and again just before our disembarkation, only to discover "no messages."

With still no word from Bassem, we headed to the airport for our 6:00 p.m. flight. I phoned his office twice from the airport before our departure but was told both times, "The minister is in a meeting."

I now wondered if my entire effort to reach out to Bassem was resonating with him at all. Linda could sense my frustration, but I struggled to put on a bright face. I didn't want to put a damper on what was otherwise an exceptional first venture into the world of cruising.

Oh well, I tried to convince myself. *Maybe this is a sign that I should stick with just one venture at a time! At least my friend Bassem was aware that I had made every effort to help.*

We had no choice but to head home. So I tucked my briefcase into the overhead bin as we settled into our seats for the eight-hour flight to Singapore.

As we headed toward June, winter was fully upon us. Along with dark, cold, rainy days, winter in New Zealand featured high Pacific Ocean winds that swept right through the isthmus of Auckland and on over the Tasman Sea toward Australia.

It was an especially blustery June morning when Linda donned her down parka and left our apartment to board the Oliver Bay ferry. Following a twelve-minute ride across the bay, she was to make her way on foot, as usual, to her psychotherapy office on Queen Street in Auckland's Central Business District.

Some hours later, two Auckland policemen pulled up in front of our Calliope Road flat. I spotted their police car from our front window, quickly ran to the computer, moved all the "Banjo" files into a folder marked "Music," hid the extra photographs in a book, and slipped the dossier under the mattress. I waited for the doorbell to ring.

Instead, there was a knock. As I walked down the stairs and opened the ground-level door, one of the officers greeted me somberly, "Mr. Kadison?"

"Yes, sir, what is this about?" I tried to contain my nervousness, certain they had come to look into my contact with Bassem.

"I'm afraid we have some bad news for you. May we come in?"

The Oliver Bay ferry terminal was built into the side of a Devonport hill. It consisted of a wooden upper deck at the end of a parking lot near the top of the hill and a metal stairway that led down to a railless floating pier at water level. The floating pier was held in place by four ancient round wooden pylons, one in each corner. The pier would ride up and down as the tide rose and fell.

According to the Auckland Ferry Company's standard operating procedure, waiting passengers were to stand on the upper deck until the arriving ferry was safely moored to the pier below. They would then walk down the metal stairway to the floating pier and board the boat once it had been safely secured. A ferry company employee would gesture to the waiting passengers to indicate it was safe to walk down the stairs.

But on this tempestuous day, the lone ferry company employee was busy down below, struggling to tie each arriving ferry to the wildly tossing lower pier. The passengers waiting above, eager to get to work, grew impatient. Seeing the open stairway before them, Linda and a few fellow passengers inched their way down to the pier in anticipation of seizing the best seats for the choppy ride across the bay.

As the ferry captain struggled mightily to maneuver his boat into a docking position, the vessel delivered a violent jolt. Linda, standing now on the floating dock, strove to keep her balance while clutching her open umbrella in one hand and securing her purse with the other. But when the ship gave another powerful thrust, she slipped sideways off the dock and fell against the bow of the vessel. She slammed her shoulder on the wood-trim molding and tumbled into the frigid harbor waters. Her down parka quickly dragged her under.

The employee frantically stretched over the watery gap to grab a lifesaver from the bow. He threw it out in her direction, but she did not surface. He dove in headlong to save her, but the turbulent waters only made matters worse. After two more dives, he finally brought up her limp body and lifted her to the captain waiting on the platform. Both tried valiantly to resuscitate her. But it was to no avail.

I hadn't cried in years, but the tears flowed easily now as the policemen related the details of Linda's accident. I had been on the other side of the living room many times, conveying similarly sad news to a number of families over the years. But now that I was the mourner, I lost my composure. I simply could not control myself.

After waiting quietly for some time while I sat sobbing with my face buried in my hands, one of the officers cleared his throat and then spoke up.

"Sir, we will need you to come with us to the morgue to identify your wife's body. In the meantime, is there anyone we should telephone?"

"Yes, please," I managed to say, slowly regaining my composure. "Leon Berman of the Hebrew Burial and Benevolent Society. The number is near the telephone. He'll know what to do."

At the morgue, they showed me only her face, battered and bruised and bloated. I tried to contain my sobbing in such a public place but had a good cry once I sat back at the wheel of our car.

I made my way over to the Waikumete Cemetery office and phoned Rabbi Matthew Isaacson to ask him to fly up from Wellington to conduct the funeral. I also phoned the children and arranged for them to fly down to Auckland and stay for the seven days of shiva following the funeral. When they left, I was more disoriented than before.

I floundered about in a daze for a number of weeks following the accident, going through the motions of my work, inviting guest speakers from the congregation to take my place on the bima.

"You already know how to conduct the service, and your talk needn't be anything fancy," I assured them. "Just speak out of your own experience, and tell us how you relate to the Torah portion of the week."

After a month, I returned to my pulpit, but I broke down in tears at the slightest mention of "love" or "companionship" or "sorrow" in the liturgy.

The greatest challenge came in leading the congregation in the recitation of the mourner's Kaddish. After a couple of ill-starred attempts, I decided to call Leon Berman up to the bima to lead them.

Without Linda by my side, I slowly began to realize my pulpit days were numbered.

The High Holy Days of 2007 represented the beginning of a significant transition in my life. I had just begun the thirtieth year of my rabbinate. But it was getting harder to remain upbeat and optimistic in the pulpit. I was also finding it more and more difficult to write inspiring sermons. In my abject sorrow, I vowed never to board another cruise ship without Linda by my side.

So I resolved to retire the following April at the age of sixty and cast my fate to the wind thereafter. That meant the upcoming month of September would mark my final High Holy Days as a pulpit rabbi.

Make it a good one, I told myself as I sat down to write my Rosh Hashanah sermon.

With Linda's passing and my decision to retire, I had become considerably less attentive to Bassem ibn Talal and his Al-Quds hotel murder investigation. I remembered the proverb "Justice delayed . . . justice denied." Even though the three "Most Wanted" photos continued to appear on his website, I sadly came to realize that the further the assassination faded into the background, the less likely anything would be done to apprehend the perpetrators. So I tried to put the whole Banjo Braham episode behind me once and for all.

Of course, that's when I heard from Bassem again. A letter from Dubai arrived in early October, but it made no apology for the long delay. By then, it was nine months since the assassination and nearly six months since our trip to Dubai.

Shalom aleichem, Rabbi Jonathan,

I was very sorry to hear the news of your tragic loss. May the memory of your beloved wife, Linda, be a blessing unto you.

Please bring all the evidence you have in your possession to our next meeting, which I recommend we schedule here in Dubai in November—at the expense of my ministry, of course. We can also discuss other financial matters. I will be much less busy at that time of year before the tourist season begins.

Bassem ibn Talal
Lieutenant General Head of General Security for the Emirate of Dubai, Minister Bassem ibn Talal

I immediately noted the glaring absence of Bassem's personal signature on this latest communiqué. Instead, the letter bore a signature stamp above his title. That was all. A terse, businesslike letter from my old friend, not even signed in his own hand.

Hmm, I thought to myself as I read the letter again. *Something has changed. I need to be very careful now.*

I made a few inquiries, nonetheless, the following day and the next. Although Bassem had requested I come to Dubai for our meeting, I began to search for an alternative. I discovered that Singapore—which was tightly controlled by the Singapore Police Force under the direction of the prime minister—would be a safe halfway meeting place. There were frequent nonstop flights to and from Auckland, as well as to and from Dubai, as I had already experienced. I anticipated Bassem's reluctance to meet in a neutral location. I hoped to compensate that with the fact that Singapore was a little closer to Dubai than to Auckland.

On the third day, I wrote a formal letter in response. Absent were some of the friendly pleasantries we had exchanged in our previous communiqués. I was cautious.

Dear Minister ibn Talal:

Thank you for your recent letter. I will be happy to meet you at Singapore Changi Airport. Might I suggest the date of Wednesday, November 28? I notice there are five nonstop flights from Dubai that day.

I realize this is not the most convenient arrangement for you, and I appreciate your offer of compensation. However, I believe it is best to meet in a neutral location that is also no more than a few hours' flight

from Auckland. I still have my considerable congrega-
tional duties to perform and cannot be absent from the
community for more than a couple of days.

 I am a member of the Constellation Alliance Club
and can arrange to have a meeting room set aside for us
in the club area at Changi Airport that day.

 Minister ibn Talal, I hope with all sincerity that
we can meet to conclude this matter. Please, therefore,
kindly send me your flight details at your earliest con-
venience.

Yours most sincerely,
Jonathan
Rabbi Jonathan Kadison

I signed it "Jonathan" in my own hand above my typewritten full name, wishing to preserve a modicum of the friendly bond we had once shared and, I hoped, would share yet again.

 An answer finally came back in mid-October.

Dear Rabbi,

I accept your invitation to meet on 28 November in
Changi Airport in Singapore. I hope to arrive on one
of the direct flights, inshallah.

Bassem ibn Talal
Lieutenant General Head of General Security for the
Emirate of Dubai, Minister Bassem ibn Talal

Once again, the letter bore a signature stamp followed by his printed title. Perhaps with his star rising in the international firmament, he no longer had time to read and sign his outgoing mail after he dictated it; perhaps his secretary took care of that. With this rationalization, I began to regain my optimism for a productive conclusion to this saga.

My hope was strengthened when I checked the Dubai police website one last time before my departure. I discovered that all references to and accounts of the Al-Quds affair—the videos Bassem had so carefully pieced together, the written account of the incident, even the "Most Wanted" photos—had all been removed.

Aha, I thought to myself. *Bassem is shutting down that part of his website. He knows he'll soon have in his hand all the evidence he needs to bring the matter to its rightful conclusion.*

I departed Auckland Airport at 1:30 p.m. on Tuesday, November 27, and arrived at 7:00 p.m. at Singapore Changi Airport. I boarded a cab and checked in at 8:00 p.m. at the Riverside Hotel on Havelock Road.

I planned to get a decent night's sleep and then return to the airport in plenty of time to meet the first of five nonstop flights from Dubai. It was an overnight flight scheduled to arrive at 5:30 a.m. I fell asleep thinking about the next day's meeting with my old friend Bassem.

CHAPTER XXX.

 SINGAPORE. 2008.

He will fly away like a dream and not be found.

JOB 20:8

I did not see the needle as she jabbed it into me, so absorbed was I in the abrupt change in her visage. Will I come out of this? *I now wondered, struggling to seize hold of a single unraveling thread of consciousness . . .*

Ah, yes—now I'm remembering. The meeting never happened. I sat in the arrivals area from 5:30 a.m. to past midnight waiting for him to appear. But Bassem was nowhere to be found. I thought we had agreed that Singapore would be an acceptable meeting place. So where was he?

And who was she—that woman, the one who had been right here at this table? Was I in a dream? I tried to pinch myself to see, but I couldn't.

Did all that happen just now? It seems like a lifetime ago.

I was beginning to hear voices now, real voices, getting louder, getting closer, and getting clearer.

When they arrived in the middle of the night, the Singapore Police found my limp body slumped over the table in the River Garden Coffee House. I was barely breathing but fully conscious now. I could not move a muscle, not even to speak, so they carried me to a sofa in the manager's room behind the front desk. The chief called for an ambulance.

"Why did you not phone us earlier?" Chief Andrew Liu inquired of the bartender.

"The lady he was with came up to me and said, 'He just needs to sleep it off.' I was surprised because he had had only one drink, but who knows what he was drinking before? So I left him alone."

"Jay, check his pupils," the chief instructed his sergeant.

"There is a pupillary response, Chief. He's responding to my light," I heard the sergeant say.

They went through my pockets and evidently found only a few Singapore dollars, some New Zealand dollars, and some mixed change.

"No wallet? No passport? No driver's license? No ID? No room key? Who is this man?" the chief thundered, calling out to no one particular.

"They're in my briefcase!" I wanted to shout out, but I couldn't make a sound.

"His name is Jonathan Kadison," the night manager chimed in meekly. "He lives in Devonport—that is, Auckland, New Zealand. He checked in with a New Zealand passport Tuesday night and was due to check out this morning."

"Maybe he left it all in his room, Chief," Jay offered.

"*So go there!*" the chief roared.

I could hear two sets of footsteps briskly walking off: probably Jay and the night manager, who would let him into my room.

Before long, they returned.

"The room has been completely overturned, Chief," Jay reported. "It's a disaster area. We searched through the mess very carefully but couldn't find much. No wallet. None of the other items. The bartender said he had a briefcase, but we couldn't find one. Just this American passport and—"

"He's an American?" the night manager interrupted. "But he carried a New Zealand passport!"

"Yes, sir," Jay replied.

"Maybe he has *two* passports," the chief chimed in dismissively.

Still unable to move or speak, all I could do is let my mind reel. Did she steal my identity along with my dignity? Did she take my coveted New Zealand passport? Was my dossier on Banjo gone now too? If only I could speak up and explain. On the other hand, what could I say?

"We also found this prescription vial and this liquid—both in his name," Jay said. "It looks like eye drops."

"Give me those," the chief said. "Let's see—Soma and eserine. Plus alcohol at the bar. I'm beginning to see what happened here."

"What are you thinking, Chief?" Jay asked.

"I think it's sux."

Jay must have been a bit taken aback by the chief's utterance, but he didn't dare show it. "Yes, sir. It certainly does, sir. Just like the Americans say."

"No, Jay. It is 'sux.' Suxamethonium. It's such a long name, they just call it 'sux.' It's a drug. It paralyzes the body, every muscle in the body. But it usually doesn't last this long. So I'm thinking it must have been enhanced by one or more of these prescriptions. Be sure to give these prescriptions to the EMTs when they arrive. And tell them, 'The chief thinks he has been given sux.' Say it like that."

Good work, Chief, I thought. My soma is always with me when I'm under pressure. And the eye drops help me manage my new affliction, glaucoma. These two trusty companions must not have liked what she had in that needle.

"Let me see your computer," the chief requested of the hotel manager. "I want to look up more about this Jonathan Kadison." There was some typing and a pause. "He's a rabbi. Auckland Progressive Hebrew Congregation. Here's a photo. Yes. This is him. I've got a phone number. Good. Excuse me for a minute, everyone."

The chief walked off into the corner of the manager's room, speaking quietly on his mobile phone.

The chief then shouted to the group, "What time is it in New Zealand?"

The night manager yelled back, "They are four hours ahead of us."

"Okay," said the chief. "It's 8:45 a.m. there now. Let's see if anyone answers."

I strained to hear what the chief was saying.

"Hello. Is this the Auckland Progressive, uh, Hebrew Congregation? Good. Good morning. This is Chief Andrew Liu with Singapore Police Force. Yes. Do you know where your rabbi is? Yes, I said Singapore. No, he's alive, but he is, uh, injured and—pardon me? His apartment? In Devonport? What happened? When? Yesterday? He was here yesterday. What does *ransacked* mean? I'm not familiar with the term. Ah yes—turned upside down. That seems to be the pattern with this fellow."

He muttered the last part under his breath, but I was hearing better now. By this point, I was beginning to put the pieces of the puzzle together.

"So what was taken from his apartment?" the chief continued. "Computer. Photo albums. Photos scattered about. Papers scattered about. Any money? No? Jewelry? No? Hmm. Okay. He will be in Mount Elizabeth Hospital. But don't call him yet. I'm hoping he'll come out of this in a few days. But even then, he may not be himself. There may be some, uh, damage, so tread lightly, please. Yes, you can telephone him then. In a few days. Yes, you can send flowers. Okay. Please let me know if you have any more information about the burglary. Again, I'm Chief Andrew Liu. Is my mobile phone number showing up on your end? Yes, yes, I will. Good-bye."

At that very moment, the ambulance crew walked through the door. They lifted me up, placed me on their gurney, hooked me up to oxygen, and then set me down inside the ambulance. They drew my blood, though it must have been hard to find a vein.

As the ambulance drove off, I realized I might never know who that woman was, whom she worked for, or what their intentions were. I don't think they intended to kill me; I think they just wanted to take whatever evidence I had and move me out of the way. And my IDs? Well, they probably had a good forger on staff.

And there in my drug-induced silence, I was beginning to understand what I think old people fear most—at least, what *I* was beginning to fear most on the verge of becoming a senior citizen. It wasn't death. No. That realization surprised me.

Rather, I was aware that they had consigned me to a fate that was, in some ways, more agonizing than death. They—whoever they were—had rendered me irrelevant. Superfluous. Extraneous. Marginalized. Past my "use by" date. That's what I was now becoming. If I survived this, I would become invisible, a "pensioner" with diminishing impact on the world as it passed by before me.

That's how the future now looked to me—and *that*, to me, was absolutely terrifying.

By the time I arrived at Mount Elizabeth Hospital, I could hold my eyes open for a couple of seconds. Within a couple of hours, I would begin to make primitive vocal sounds. But I had become so disoriented that I wasn't aware of the day of the week or the day of the month. I couldn't recall any of this until later, when my kind nurse brought in a copy of the *Straits Times*, the English-language daily.

She held it up for me as I read the front page, a process that must have taken quite a long time, as my eyes kept closing. After a while, she opened it to the next page, where the international news could be found.

A bold headline on the right side of page 3, above the fold, brought it all into focus for me:

ISRAEL DELEGATION MAKES HISTORIC VISIT TO DUBAI:
FULL DIPLOMATIC RELATIONS,
DIRECT AIR SERVICE ON AGENDA

I closed my tired old eyes, mumbled "Go" to the nurse, and fell back on the pillow. I tried, but I couldn't yet manage to bring a smile of satisfaction to my face. But it would come.

IN MEMORIAM

JONATHAN KOPSTEIN

1952–77

ACKNOWLEDGMENTS

Special thanks go to my patient readers and advisors: Alex, Andy, Barbara, Beanie, Dani, David, Joel, Leslie, Mason, Pam, Sheri, Tal, Tisa, and Tony.

I could not have completed this project without the selfless support and brilliant insights of my lovely and loving wife, Patti. She has been right by my side throughout this incredible journey.

Thank you, Laura Drew, for the exquisite book design from cover to cover.

A special thank-you to Leo Bonamy and his capable assistant, Desmond, for our marvelous website.

Thank you to the remarkable folks at Beaver's Pond Press: Hanna, Lily, and Tom. And most especially to my talented editor, Angela Wiechmann, whose creativity, wisdom, patience, resourcefulness, and enthusiasm were invaluable.

Finally, to you, my reader. You have all made it all worthwhile!